SETTLE DOWN

Stephanie Perry Moore

SADDLEBACK
EDUCATIONAL PUBLISHING

CHEER DRAMA

Always Upbeat

Keep Jumping

Yell Out

Settle Down

Shake It

SADDLEBACK
EDUCATIONAL PUBLISHING
www.sdlback.com

ISBN-13: 978-1-61651-887-5
ISBN-10: 1-61651-887-1
eBook: 978-1-61247-621-6

Printed in Guangzhou, China
0712/CA21201000

16 15 14 13 12   1 2 3 4 5

To Jenell Clark, Chandra Dixon, and Sarah Lundy

You all inspire me. I truly am grateful that you all are my friends. Keep on living life to the fullest. Your spunk, sass, and style motivates me to be the best me I can be and never settle for less. May every reader long to speak truth and continually strive to be awesome.

Stay amazing … I love you!

ACKNOWLEDGEMENTS

It is good to have backbone: not be pushed over and not care what others think of you. You should be a leader and not a follower. You should move to the beat of your own drum. You should walk with pep in your step.

However, being too carefree has consequences. Having a bad reputation works against you in life. Be tough, but not pigheaded. Be stern, but not rude. Be daring, but don't make dumb choices or put yourself in dangerous situations. You might feel grown, but don't rush life. Settle down and make wise choices. Bottom line: don't put yourself in compromising positions. You do have a rep to protect.

Here are massive thanks to all who help chill, think, and create.

For my parents, Dr. Franklin and Shirley Perry Sr., thanks for teaching me to settle down and enjoy every day.

Acknowledgements

For my publisher, especially Ashley Thompson, thanks for helping me settle down and make a series that can make a difference.

For my extended family: brother, Dennis Perry, mother-in-law, Ann Redding, brother-in-Christ, Jay Spencer, godmother, Marjorie Kimbrough, and goddaughter, Danielle Lynn, thanks for getting me to settle down and know family is important in life.

For my assistants: Joy Spencer and Keisha King, thanks for helping me settle down, not panic, and know I'm on point with the story.

For my friends whom I love to pieces: Leslie Perry, Lakeba Williams, Nicole Smith, Torian Colon, Loni Perriman, Kim Forest, Vickie Davis, Kim Monroe, Jamell Meeks, Michele Jenkins, Lois Barney, Perlicia Floyd, Veronica Evans, Laurie Weaver, Taiwanna Brown-Bolds, Matosha Glover, Yolanda Rodgers-Howsie, Dayna Fleming, Denise Gilmore, and Deborah Bradley, thanks for caring and getting me to settle down and appreciate the joy of meaningful relationships.

For my teens: Dustyn, Sydni, and Sheldyn, thanks for giving your mom time to settle down and write, write, write.

For my husband, Derrick, thanks for loving me so much and helping me daily to settle down and work on my craft.

For my new readers, thanks for trying my novel and settling down to get something out of the tale.

And to my Savior, thanks for blessing me and allowing me to settle down, knowing I'm right where You want me to be.

CHAPTER 1

Lower Standards

Eva, you did so good, girl," my mom cheered. We had just placed second out of eight teams in our cheerleading competition.

My father came to my other side, kissed my cheek, and said, "Yeah, Eva, you were amazing."

"Eva, you were the best!" my twin sister, Ella, screamed.

Having the three of them say something great about me at the same moment made me feel better than I had felt in a long time. See, I was known as take-no-prisoners Eva Blount, a salty, sassy, and forward junior at Lockwood High School. Everyone knew not to mess with me. I spoke my mind. I did my thing. I held my own.

At that moment, I was feeling tough, but I realized there were things in my life that truly mattered to me. One thing high on the list was my family. We had been estranged for years. Though my dad lived with us until I was five, he and my mother were never married. As a little girl, I did not know why he left us, and now that I am practically a woman, I realize he was trapped by my mom early on.

He came to Clark Atlanta University to get an education. Like most young men, he was also looking for a good time. He found that and more with my mom. She was looking for a meal ticket, and at the time he was perfect. They were both young, and the consequences of their affair were not just one baby but two. While he stuck around initially, trying to make life work, he wanted more than the projects could offer. As soon as we were not toddlers, he was out.

Like a fisherman throwing a line in the water looking for a catch, I said, "Let's all go get something to eat." They went for it. "Time to celebrate."

"Your dad probably has to get back to Samantha," my mom said, giving my dad an out.

"No, I can get something to eat. Let's do it," my dad replied, really making me happy.

Samantha was my dad's pregnant wife-to-be. Supposedly, she was more my dad's type than my mom: an educated woman with style. My mom had a little weight on her. I vowed to never let myself go like that because back in the day her body was slamming like mine. Now, while still attractive, she herself wanted to shed some pounds.

I told my folks I needed to go get my bag. My twin, Ella, came with me. We were thrilled at the thought of eating with both of our folks.

"I wanted to be out there with you guys so bad," she said.

"Please, I was just glad you were here to watch it."

"I gotta get better by regional and state," Ella declared.

I defended, "Only if you're stronger."

"I go back to the doctor on Monday," she said.

My sister gave me a hug with the arm that wasn't bandaged up. A few days back, we were at a party after a football game, and a bullet grazed her arm. As horrible as that was, she was very lucky. She instinctively pushed her boyfriend out of the way—dumbest crap in the world. Though Ella and I looked identical, we were total opposites in personality. In my opinion, she was a pushover. If she could please the world, she would.

I had backbone, and while my sister and a couple other of my close girlfriends thought they were all in love, I loved myself. I figured out a long time ago when I did not have my dad there to hold me through my nightmares that I was going to have to be there for me. Guys, in my opinion, were good for just a few things: a free meal, some quick cash, and a good feeling. They liked my body, wanted to hit it and be gone. If I liked them, two could play at that game.

Later at dinner, we were actually having a good time. Realizing that life was precious and that we were blessed to have Ella still alive softened all our hearts.

Without thinking about distractions, a distraction came. My dad's cell phone vibrated. He was so in to talking to my mom that he was not paying attention. I just picked it up and noticed it was Samantha.

"When are you coming home?" the text read.

Instinctively, I typed, "Out with my family, not sure."

Quickly she texted back, "What do you mean, your family???"

Before anyone noticed, I texted back, "Evan and our unborn child are not my only kids. I'll be there when I get there."

I smiled slyly as I erased the series of texts. I wondered how mad Samantha probably was as she read each word. She was *not* going to ruin my family dinner. Ha!

My dad could do better than Samantha. She might have a nice career and look all cute and stuff, but she was a selfish witch. My dad wanted to try to get to know us. At first I did not want to bond, but my sister did. She actually moved in with them. Samantha was threatened so much that she told my sister it would be better if she moved out, and sweet little Ella complied.

When I saw my dad touch my mom's hand, I gasped. I know it probably didn't mean anything, but it could. Samantha just had to be dealt with.

I said, "Hey, Dad, you talked about wanting to get to know me some. This weekend I know

Mom wants Ella to rest up. Maybe I could get away and come and hang out with you guys. Would that be okay?"

He turned and looked at me and said, "Eva, you want to hang out with me? Spend some time with Evan and Samantha? Really?"

The way he was saying it was like he thought I detested his other family. Actually, I did. They were a bother to me, but I had a plan.

So I put on a smiling face and said, "Yeah, I want to come."

"That would be great," he said. I could not stop smiling.

Later, he took me by my mom's to get my overnight bag. Ella looked like she did not want me to go. My mom looked like she wanted me to be tough since I was feisty, like her.

My mom hugged me tight and said, "Please, don't get into it with that lady. I know she can't push you around like she does Ella, but don't start World War III."

"I gotcha, Mom. I can handle this."

As soon as we stepped into my dad's place, Samantha looked furious. But, I knew how to play her game. The key was, I knew how to play *her*.

"Samantha, hey, thanks for letting m
over," I crowed.

She was the one making my dad mad.
Watching her frowning and rolling her eyes had
me laughing on the inside. Yup, I had his wife-to-
be just the way I wanted her. She made Ella look
like the bad one. Now she had met her match.

While the two of them argued, my little
brother tugged on my jacket. He was so cute, but
he was the enemy. I could not like him. I wanted
my dad back. He called me Ella.

"No, Evan, I'm Eva."

"Ella, Ella," he repeated.

As much as I did not want to like the little
boy, hating that my dad had another kid, I was
not a bad person. So I picked him up and explained that I was his other big sister. I guess
I did not twirl him around the way Ella did because he looked a little disappointed. That was
fine with me because I was not trying to baby-sit.

Later that evening when my dad was putting Evan to sleep, I walked in on Samantha
addressing some wedding invitations. She was
too happy for my taste. I was the pin ready to
burst her bubble.

I startled her when I said, "You might be wasting your time doing all that. Once my dad sees who you *really* are, all this wedding planning and marriage stuff is probably going to be over."

"Why are you even here?" she stood up and said, looking like she could drop her baby any minute.

Messing with her, I re-quoted the text she thought was from my dad and said, "Evan and our unborn child are not my only kids."

"You're not planning to stay, are you?" Samantha asked, looking pretty desperate.

"If I do decide to, you're not going to run me away like you did my sister."

"I didn't mean for it—"

"You know what? Just save it," I said, cutting her off. "No need to pretend we like each other. No need to think we want the same things, and certainly no need for you to get it twisted. I am *not* Ella."

I turned and walked away with her tongue. I knew how to deal with women like her. Heck, I was *one* of them. Now that I realized I loved my dad, I was not just going to let her keep him from me. Game was on.

"Eva, you better hurry up. We're going to miss the bus," Ella said to me as if it was her job to be my mom. "Come on, girl, dang."

While I was super excited she was still alive and that the bullet only grazed her arm, there were times that the things she did just got under my skin and on my nerves. I did not operate on CP Time. I was not chronically late for everything. I was on Eva Time. What was the difference? Well, on Colored People Time you always seemed to be rushing and just could not make it there when something starts. On Eva Time you know what is up. Your intention is to make an entrance, or you just do not care about being late.

"You don't have to jump all down my throat," I said.

"I was just trying to make sure you knew what time it was. You're not even ready, and the bus could be early. You know how that lady is."

"Yup, that's why I'm not depending on her. Just take care of you, and I'll see you in school," I responded a little calmer because I did not want to fuss with my sister.

My mom worked so hard. She was already gone. My ride was coming from another person. A fine, new guy named Rico was going to pick me up. I met him at the party last week at Wax's place. Not only was Rico handsome, but he was mature. He was not young like the little high school boys at Lockwood. Rico was a man, a college dude, and maybe I was too much like my mom. Maybe there was something about college men that made me want to hook them by any means necessary.

Rico honked. I would have preferred him to come to the door. Who knows? Maybe he would have got a little surprise kiss. Though I had just met him, he seemed really cool. Even though when *I* got to college I certainly was not going to be hanging out at no high school gig, I still thought he had it going on.

"Why didn't you come inside?"

"I didn't need any moms checking me out or nothing," Rico stated, misunderstanding.

"My mom's at work."

"Oh, I can turn this car around, baby."

"No, we might as well keep on going now," I commented. It was way too fast to be expecting what I knew he was thinking.

"I got tinted windows. I was going to take you back to my place and let you see what you're in store for in a couple of years."

"Well, you were late coming to get me."

"I had to go take care of a lil' something. Plus, we're together now. Let's be adventurous," Rico said with a wink.

He parked the car in the front of the school. He leaned over and stroked my face with the back of his hand. Rico smelled so good. Then he leaned over me and reclined my seat. He took his hand and started going up my shirt.

I jerked to the side and snapped, "You can't do that."

"Why can't I? Am I being too rough?"

Then he started touching me gently. "Like that?"

"No, we're in front of my school."

"Yeah, but school's already started. I'll send you to class once I ring your bell."

His lips touched mine. He had a forcefulness that lured me in. He knew what he was doing, and he wanted me. When the actual school bell rang, I started kissing his neck, and he was moaning.

I said, "Not now, baby, another time. Let's get to know each other."

"I know you just fine," he replied. He started to handle me a little rougher.

He proceeded to enjoy himself just a little. Thankfully, there was a knock at my window. Somebody had my back. Except I was startled when I saw Dr. Sapp staring back real upset. Rico's windows were not tinted *that* much. I was caught making out in front of the school.

"Young man, do you attend Lockwood High School?" Dr. Sapp asked.

"Nah, man," Rico snarked.

"Well, then you best get to moving. Eva Blount, let's go," my principal demanded.

"I know, Dr. Sapp. I have to get to class. Can I say good-bye?"

"Nah, you got to get to my office."

"Dr. Sapp, come on," I said as he made me get out of the car and walk with him.

Rico took off. Dr. Sapp escorted me to his office. I had to sit and wait until my mom arrived. I knew she would not be happy.

"Eva, I just don't understand. Why would you make such bad decisions? This man could suspend you," my mom shouted in Dr. Sapp's office.

He and I could have talked through this. He did not have to call my mom. The way he was looking at her got me to thinking, there was more to why he phoned her to come in for a conference.

"This is just so hard. I'm doing all I can raising these two girls. It still seems like I'm not doing enough. Ella just got out of ISS, and then she ends up in the hospital. Now Eva's acting up," my mom vented.

Dr. Sapp got up from behind his desk. He came over to my mom and rubbed her back. I could not tell if she was faking it, wanting his sympathy to ease my punishment, or if I truly had upset her that much. I definitely could tell he was happy to console her. He handed her a tissue, and when I saw real tears, I felt bad. My mom was seriously going through it. Although my dad has stepped in and helped get the rent up to date, her plate was full. I was basically toppling it over with my poor choices.

"Do you have to suspend her, sir? Is there any way you can give her a warning? Eva's the last person who needs to be missing school. Plus they got this regional state cheerleading competition coming up. Can you help me out, please?" my mom pleaded.

Dr. Sapp smiled way big and said, "Yes, if you do something for me."

"Okay," my mom responded slowly.

Dr. Sapp was crossing the line. What was he talking about? And what was he insinuating? There was nothing my mom needed to do for him. I am not saying I wanted her to be single the rest of her life, but at least for now, I didn't want her to be available.

Now, Dr. Sapp was a good catch. He was an educated man bringing in big bank. He didn't appear to have baggage.

However, a part of me was selfish. My dad was already getting married. My twin sister was already goo-goo eyes over some football player on our team. I did not want to be alone. It was time for me and my mom to bond and hang out.

Being real, I could see Dr. Sapp was her type. Clean cut, slick with the tongue, and cool. He was not an uptight principal. He was checking her out way too much.

Stepping in, I said, "Uh, I'll take any punishment. My mom doesn't need to do anything for you."

"I wanted her to cook me one of those pecan pies she made last year. Don't think I forgot, Ms. Blount."

"Oh, you know I could do that," my mom laughed like a silly school girl.

"With Thanksgiving coming up and me being a single man and all, I gotta figure out how I'm going to eat. If I eat no turkey, I certainly want to have dessert."

My mom said, "Well, we can't have you alone on Thanksgiving."

"Oh no, no, no, I wouldn't dare intrude," he said, trying to pretend like he would not invite himself.

"Uh, if I'm not going to get in trouble, can I go to class?" I huffed.

"You sit on down here," my mom said boldly.

Dr. Sapp said, "Yeah, we're worried about you, Eva. If you need to talk to the counselor or anything like that—"

"My baby doesn't need to talk to the counselor," my mom interrupted Dr. Sapp.

"I'm just saying, Ms. Blount, your daughter is developing a reputation around here that I don't think you want. You told me last time when Ella was in here that you and I could talk. I'm keeping it real."

I folded my arms, pouted my lips, and looked out of his window. I did not give a darn what people thought about me. I was in front of the school making out because that was my choice. Girls wish they had it going on like I did. Guys salivated at the thought of wanting to knock my boots. I do not know what reputation he was talking about that was supposedly so bad, but I was fine with me.

I stood up and asked for a pass. They hesitated, but I stood firm so they could tell I was not shaken. When I got it, I left the two of them in Dr. Sapp's office, doing who knows what.

As I turned the corner to go to science, one of the stupid football players wasn't looking where he was going and bumped right into me. It was Landon King, the star wide receiver. On the field he was in control of his moves, but off the field ... he was a klutz. The boy tried too hard to be cool like Leo, Blake, and Waxton.

"Watch where you're going," I snapped. But then I looked at his face and saw he was real frazzled.

"Sorry, sorry," Landon responded, quickly going around me and heading into the boys restroom.

Landon had more muscles than I realized because he hurt my shoulder bumping into me. He was not even a defensive player, yet he was packing. For a fleeting second, I hoped he was cool.

Dr. Sapp walked my mom out to the hall and she yelled out, "Eva, you're not in class? Girl, you are working my nerves. The man's giving you a break, and you take your time."

I wanted to yell out, "Just get you some, Mom, so you will chill out."

But I was respectful. I smiled at them both and walked toward my classroom door. Looking back, seeing the way she was blushing at Dr. Sapp, bothered my very core. She tripped me out trying to act like she was disappointed in how I was acting, but truth be told, the fruit does not fall too far from the tree.

"School's out, so let me come and finish what we started this morning," Rico crooned.

"I can't, babe. I have cheerleading practice."

"Whatever, skip that," he commanded, immediately letting me know he really did not care about what I had going on in my life.

The last thing you could call me was an idiot. To him I was like a chicken. He liked my legs, breasts, and thighs. The thing was, I told him he had to pay to play. I needed to feel him a little. He had to have more than a cute body and a nice car to sample what I had to offer.

"Look, you gonna lose out if you don't let me come pick you up now," he threatened.

Needing the brother to chill, I brazenly said, "Well, I guess I'm going to lose out then because I don't like brothers who raise their voice at me and can't appreciate what I got going on. I don't know about those college girls who go to school with you, but I don't need to be with you every five minutes. And I certainly don't want someone smothering me."

"All right, Eva, I hear you. I like you, girl. You're feisty. I'ma have to tame you though. Them little high school boys let you run things."

"If I wanted to be with a high school boy, I'd be with one," I uttered with confidence. "At the same time, if I wanted to be on a leash, I'd bark like a dog to your every beck and call. However, that's just not me, Rico. So if we need to squash this and end it now ..."

Wising up, he said, "I said I got you."

"You said you got me, but then you go on and keep pressing me."

"Nah, babe, I hear you. After cheerleading practice then, I'll pick you up."

"No, ugh, bye," I groaned. I looked at the cell like there was a stupid person on the other end.

"Wait, wait, wait," he begged before I could hang up.

"I've just been thinking about you, babe," he said. "That's all. I can't even keep my mind on my school books. The professor is just talking, and all I'm doing is seeing images of fine Eva Blount, and now you won't let a brother see you when he wants to. You know how to control my mind. Do your thing, and I'll check back in with you," he said. I guess he realized that he was ticking me off.

"Cool," I stated.

I guess I had a thing for older men because on the way to the locker room to change for cheerleading practice, I saw a very handsome substitute teacher. He had to be in his early thirties. He had a little goatee and looked like he lifted weights. His muscles were just that defined in his shirt. I knew if Dr. Sapp saw me fawning, he would tell him it was inappropriate showing all that to us high school girls. Our math teacher was out on maternity leave, and I could not wait until the next day when I had Mrs. Byrd's class because her sub could teach me a lot.

It was interesting though. Landon seemed to be having an intense conversation with him. We all knew our real teacher left too much work for us to get done, but Landon did not need to vent to the substitute. That was twice in one day I saw him upset. The team was 7–0. What did he have to complain about?

I was trying not to do any running. We were punished if we were late and had to run laps around the gym. I looked down at my watch and saw that it was almost time for us to report to Coach Woods on the gym floor. I was actually looking forward to practice. With the momentum we had a week back, it was time to place at regional so that we could qualify for state.

When I got in the locker room, I could not wait to tell my girls about the sub whose name badge read Mr. Gunn. The five of us loved getting a laugh off of good-looking men. I liked giving the four of them a hard time: my twin sister, Ella; Charli, the captain of our cheerleading squad; Hallie, who was loud but always there to help everyone; and Randal, the shy one of our group. You never knew what Randal was thinking because she never said a word. Before I could get to them, I was shocked by what I heard.

Randal said, "So I just need you guys to give me some pointers. I mean, all of y'all have a man. Charli you're with Brenton,"

"Uh-huh," Hallie uttered sarcastically.

Ella said, "Why is that a big deal? She's with Brenton, right? Did I miss something?"

Hallie explained, "Girl, the night you got shot, Charli was all sad and crying. Well, Brenton wasn't the one who comforted her. It was Blake."

I actually saw them together myself, but I didn't pay it any attention. Charli and Hallie were real cool. Charli probably told her more than she wanted the rest of us to know. However, with Hallie's big mouth, now we all knew.

"No, it's not like that at all. I like Brenton a lot. He's my guy." Charli paused. "It's just that Blake and I have a long history and being in his arms … Ugh, I can't explain it."

"See, that's what I'm talking about," Randal declared.

"Here you are tripping over two guys, and I can't even get one. Ella, you and I used to hang, and I couldn't even sit with you to make sure you recuperated well because every break Leo got he was trying to play doctor. I didn't think I wanted a boyfriend, but I think I do now."

Randal needed to not be so down on herself. Just as I was about to step to her and give her some advice, I was frozen in my tracks. My girl called out my name.

"Eva."

"And?" Charli interjected in a snarky tone.

"Eva has all the guys here checking her out. I'm in classes with her. Trust me, she has the boys on lock. She's so cold and mean, but they still want to carry her books. You know what I'm saying, *carry her books*. My body's not like yours,"

Randal said to my sister, alluding that my body was also tight. "But maybe I need to show off what I have just a little bit more. You know, wear more revealing clothes like Eva. The three of you guys have somebody. Eva's got a ton of choices."

"Do you think they wanna get with her? Really get with her?" Charli insinuated.

"I don't know; I'm just saying," Randal replied.

"Think revealing and all that stuff," Charli said, trying to make a point. "Ella has a man, and Eva has boys falling all over her. Which one do you want? Because if you want to know how to get a boyfriend, you need to be talking to us, not Eva."

"Yeah, somebody said she was in front of the school this morning having sex in a car and got caught by Dr. Sapp."

Hallie liked spreading gossip. I knew Charli loved getting under my skin. Hallie was her little puppet.

I had to brace myself when my sister said, "I love Eva to death—you know that—but you're right, her reputation is horrible. Sometimes people look at me, thinking I'm her. I want to go off on them and say, 'Get your head out of the gutter,' but I can't be too mad at them because Eva puts herself in those situations, thinking her body can control men. I'm just scared because one day she's gonna get with the wrong one."

"So you think my style is cool? I don't need to be more out there," Randal asked.

"No!" all three of them shouted together.

"Huh?" Randal asked.

Charli added, "Being more out there like Eva is tired. And, girl, your style is tidy and fresh. Keep it that way."

"Girl, my sister is not dirty," Ella laughed.

"I'm not saying she's dirty. That's not what I'm saying."

Ella said, "Well, what are you saying?"

"I'm saying Randal's just fine. I'm saying what we're all saying. Eva's too provocative, flaunting everything she's got in front of guys all the time. Randal will catch the right guy without lower standards."

CHAPTER 2

Relax Baby

Okay, calm down, Eva," I said to myself, truly pissed off that my sister and my girlfriends were blasting me.

They thought I was too raunchy, but that wasn't my problem. My problem was that they didn't have enough nerve to say it to my face. They waited until they were alone and turned Randal against me. With her weak little behind, whatever they said, she went for. Yeah, she should show a little bit of skin when trying to get a guy's eye to turn her way. Like any guy wants to look at somebody covered up like a nun.

I paced back and forth, wondering if I should go confront them or keep all this frustration bottled up inside. The latter was not healthy at all. We were cheerleaders together, trying to get ready for regional and state competitions. The way I felt right now, I would not flip at all. I would not hold up any stunts. I would simply let them fall.

However, there was a major glitch in my whole not-caring scenario. I wanted the trophy just as much as any of them. I had not put in all this time, tightened up my own skills, and worked hard to pull up my grades to be a detriment to the team. So I had a huge dilemma because I had too much pride in myself to let whatever mean comments they wanted to say about me slide.

I opened up the locker room door to step out and get some water, thinking that would calm me down. However, I saw my girls' guys, Leo, Amir, and Brenton, heading my way. I guess they were going to their own locker room to change.

I looked down and saw a wooden block that was keeping the door from closing completely. I probably kicked it in the way without realizing it. An idea came to my mind. I opened the door fully, put the door stopper in tightly, went over to a bench, and started undressing. If their tails thought I was fast, then whatever. I might as well clearly go for that title.

I turned my back to the door, lifted my sweatshirt over my head, and started moving my body slowly to the left and to the right. I remembered I wore my low rise briefs, and they were mad sexy. Quickly, I pulled down my jeans. When I could feel the boys breathing through the door, I took off my T-shirt only leaving me in a bra and underwear. I pretended to fall forward over the bench.

"Ouch, oh," I screamed.

I knew if I screamed loud enough, the boys and the girls would come and try to help me. When no one was picking me up, I bent down further. I looked between my legs and saw them still standing there, looking stupid.

"Help me, Leo, please," I called out helplessly.

Actually, I could have called out any of the guys' names. Maybe on the inside I was mad at my sister the most, because out of everyone, I felt she betrayed me the most. Leo quickly came to my side. When he tried to lift me up, I became dead weight so that I would fall down again.

"Oh, I'm sorry," he said, trying not to stare at my fluorescent pink bra. "Brenton, y'all help me get her up."

"Ow," I squealed, trying to make the girls head my way so that I could make my next move.

I put my arms around Leo's neck. When he tried picking me up, I pulled him down on top of me. His head landed between my bosoms and actually touched the outline of my bra.

"What's going on here?" Hallie yelled out.

Amir grabbed her when he saw she was about to go off. I knew she was not alone. Amir tried to get her out of the area, but Charli and Randal dashed over too. They were speechless when they saw Leo and me in a compromising situation. Randal's mixed-race behind was turning red. Charli looked over at her like, *See, everything we told you about her is true.*

Leo was trying desperately to get up. We were so tangled up that he could not recover before he was caught red-handed with his hand in the cookie jar. He finally helped me to my feet and rushed over to my sister. She looked devastated. I sort of felt bad, but that's what she got for siding against me.

"It's not what you think," Leo said to Ella, but she just ran away.

Charli and Randal were pissed. Coach Woods shooed the guys away. "I don't know what's going on in here. But we've got practice. All this noise and commotion, plus having guys in my locker room is intolerable."

"Talk to *her*," Charli accused, pointing at my face with her finger.

"You had better get your finger out of my face," I threatened. "Somebody needs to talk to you. Blabbing about folks when they're not around."

"What are you talking about?" Charli questioned. "You're standing here practically naked in front of your sister's boyfriend."

I lashed back, "Like you can talk! You were practically tonguing your boyfriend's cousin."

"You don't know what you're talking about," she screamed.

I was just trying to get under her skin, and it worked. All four of these girls were so sensitive. If Randal took any pointers from them, she would not be able to get a guy. They were so irritating.

"Girls, shut your mouths and hurry up and get dressed," Coach barked. "You'll be giving me laps. So snap to it."

As soon as Coach left, Charli was back at it with me. "How could you do that to your sister?"

"The only thing I was doing was getting undressed," I replied coyly. "I didn't make the guys stop and look. Guys who supposedly would never really look my way. These studs have girlfriends. Why would they be looking anyway? Besides, you can't reel in a guy with skin," I mocked.

I wanted to tell her as much as I could so that she understood I heard them talking about me. But Charli was looking down on me from so high on her horse that she did not even realize I was spitting their conversation back at them. Randal couldn't even look at me at that point. While she had merely asked them the question about whether or not she should dress like me, she did not defend me when they told her no.

"I'm gonna go find Ella," Charli said. "I can't believe what you did to her."

"And when Brenton finds out you been seeing Blake behind his back, what do you think that's gonna do to him?" I snarled at Charli.

"You don't know what you're talking about."

"Oh, c'mon, Charli. You brag too much. I heard the word."

Charli knew she could not out-talk me. She stormed off. When she left, Randal and I were standing alone.

"You heard our conversation, didn't you?" Randal asked.

"Why do you care?" I sneered. "If I *did* hear some conversation about me, you would have had my back, right? Or would I have heard you selling me out like the rest of 'em?"

"I admire you, Eva. You know you and I are tight. You know we will always stand together. With our grades, we are two peas in a pod. On the cheer squad, we stand next to each other, but when it comes to guys, they look at you. They don't look my way. The whole thing about light-skinned girls having it all is a myth. I don't think I'm ugly, but I can never get the guys like you."

The way she was talking was like she wanted me to take sympathy on her and be all sweet to her—like she wanted to cry or wanted somebody to hand her a tissue. She didn't need to sob around me, and I was not going to comfort her.

I grabbed my stuff, slammed my locker real hard, and said, "We were supposed to be two peas in a pod till you felt too embarrassed to claim me. They bashed me and you said nothing. I didn't hear you tell them how much you admired me."

"You know I'm your friend," Randal cried. "Seriously, I love you, girl."

"With friends like you, Randal, I don't need enemies." I walked off.

I knew then she was going to bawl. She was too much of a pushover. Not my problem. She had hurt me. It was time she felt the pain back.

Randal was a cute girl. I did not know why she was alone. So what, though? You did not need to have a guy to feel like you were all that. I just proved guys were not as loyal as girls thought. I went over to the water fountain to calm down. Those four chicks were not going to get the best of me. Usually, Hallie or Charli took me home, but not today. No way was I going to be accepting a ride from them. We were through.

I said nothing to my so-called friends during practice. It was funny because in warm-ups, I actually partnered with Whitney, our co-captain, who everyone thought was a snob. However, she was a better choice to be around than any of them. They all thought something was wrong with me.

Hallie came over and said, "We are going to get some food after we change up. Anywhere you wanna go?"

I looked at her, rolled my eyes, and just walked away. She had the nerve to think that I really wanted to be around them. She acted like she didn't know what was up, which I highly doubted because all of them had big mouths. I knew Randal filled them in. Randal knew something was wrong at that point.

Trying my patience, Hallie ran in front of me and said, "We need to talk, girl. We are too tight to let the group drama build. Your sister is already so upset. You just need to apologize and—"

Cutting her off, I said, "What did you just say? You know what, Hallie, get out of my face for real. You don't have to worry about taking me home."

"Well, how are you going to get home? Is it that college boy everybody saw you with? It's all around the school that you were sexing him up on the school property," Hallie scolded.

"And we know every rumor that goes around we should believe, right?" I hinted, remembering how her name was mud last year when a senior hit it and never spoke to her again. The guy lied and said how he was proud to run a train. A cat had her tongue at that point. She could not say anything because she knew how deeply she was devastated when rumors almost ruined her sophomore year. If it was not for my smart thinking—I unleashed a rumor about how he was not able to satisfy her—the jerk never would have come clean.

Couch Woods called, "Eva, you ready to go?"

Not that I wanted it to be a secret, but I hated that she yelled out my plan in front of everybody. Going home with the coach was kinda lame. It was still better than being with any of their fake behinds.

When we got in the car, I said, "Thanks so much for taking me home."

"Oh, no problem. I'm glad you asked me for a ride. I have been meaning to spend some time with you."

"You're going the wrong way," I said to her when she turned left instead of right. "Do you remember where I live?"

"Yeah, I do, but I'm not taking you home right now. I've talked to your mom, and you and I are going to go out for dinner and a movie. How does that sound?"

I just shrugged my shoulders. I did not know what she was thinking, planning, or trying, but I was ready to go home. Then it dawned on me that Ella would show up sooner or later, and the longer I was able to stay away from dealing with her, the better.

"Yeah, that sounds great," I perked up and said. "Wait, but I don't have any money."

"Oh, no, no. It's on me," Coach said gently.

"Cool. Then I'm ready to get my grub on," I teased. "Let's go."

Why she took me to see some lame animated PG movie was beyond me. There were more interesting titles out there that I wanted to see. However, it was her dime. Her restaurant choice was a little better, thankfully. She took me to Red Lobster on Candler Road. She said I could order anything off the menu.

I wanted to ask her about her family. How was her upbringing? Did she take other girls to dinner and a movie to try to get to know them? What was the purpose of all this? I honestly started to get an attitude as we just sat there, waiting on our meal.

"Look, Eva, I want to be real with you. Can we talk, like really talk?" Again, I shrugged my shoulders.

I knew I was gonna listen to whatever she had to say. It really was not a choice on my part. Why was she asking me that dumb question?

"Why do you sometimes get so angry?" she asked. "You are such a special girl. You've got spunk. You've got style. You've goy savvy. Yet you walk around with a chip on your shoulder like the world owes you something."

The anger she mentioned rose. "You don't know my life, Coach Woods."

"Well, that's what I'm trying to figure out— why are you this way? Let's talk it out."

"I don't need fixing, and I didn't ask to come to dinner. I could have done without that pitiful movie you took me to. You just wasted your money because I was asleep. If you wanna get

the food to go, that's cool, and if you wanna forget dinner all together, I'm straight with that as
well. People don't really do anything nice for me
unless they want something, so I'm not expecting you to be any different. You ain't gonna hurt
my feelings if you wanna bounce."

"Here's the thing," Coach said. "I thought
you'd enjoy the movie, and I brought you to dinner because I'm having some issues with the
squad, and I think you're—"

"I'm what?" I said, cutting her off. "I'm the
problem."

"Well, I was going to say, I think you're the
one who can fix it."

"I don't know what you mean. I don't need
you to psychoanalyze me or try to get all up in
my head. No need to try and get me to be on your
side and stuff."

"No, you are exactly like I was when I was your
age. I did not have a silver spoon in my mouth like
Charli or Whitney. People around me had money,
and sometimes it irked me that I didn't have any.
I paid my own way through college," Coach said,
showing me she could relate just as our food finally arrived.

Opening up, I said, "Okay, so you feel me. And Charli and Whitney aren't the only ones who are crazy. Most of those girls on the squad don't even understand how tough it is to struggle. We were about to get kicked out of our apartment a couple weeks ago, and because I do things that most won't so I can eat and so I can help my mom pay bills, people look at me all strange and funny. My body is the one thing I have that makes me feel good about me."

"And so what, you gonna flaunt it all over for the world to see?" Couch Woods asked.

"Yeah," I agreed. "You said you understood. You said you used to be like me. Look at you. You're a teacher making something good with your life. All hope isn't lost for me then, right?"

"No, hope isn't lost. I got myself together because I had someone who cared and helped me turn myself around."

Putting my fork down, I said, "I'm not a drunk. I'm not on drugs. And I'm not a prostitute."

"I'm not saying that you are, but your attitude sometimes can get you into so much trouble that you're getting in your own way. That's why I'm talking to you now, because I care. I don't

want you to keep thinking that you can act anyway you want to. You don't have to always be so
tense and think people are out to get you. Every
one of those girls cares about you, especially
your sister, and she came to me crying about
some prank you pulled on her. And for what?"

"What? Ella went blabbing to you, and you
wanna take me out for dinner to get on me? Oh,
this is great. You're already on Ella's side. Everybody's always on Ella's side. She's the sweet
one. I'm the mean one."

"See, that's what I'm talking about, Eva. We
are in a restaurant, and you're sitting here acting like some ghetto girl. Calm down."

I shouted, "You're my coach, not my mama."

"Well, your mama said I can talk tough
to you, so I am. If I didn't care about you, I
wouldn't try so hard to reach you. You can't
totally brush me off because you know I'm sin-
cere. I care, even if you said that it's gonna go
in one ear and out the other. You want to have
an attitude; I'm going to have an attitude back.
We can sit here and eat this meal in silence and
not be real with each other, and you can keep
on acting like a jerk and see where it gets you.

When school started, you were the first one saying Charli was feeling herself. Well, here's the thing; you're just like her."

"Whatever."

"No, the things that bother you about her are exactly how you are. She's strong-willed and so are you. You got to her and made her change, and now you need to get to yourself."

It was so hard hearing her rant about me. Who asked her anyway? I was squirming, wanting her to hush.

She continued, "Yeah, sure I can go on and let you roll your neck, let you get smart, and throw you off the team. Honestly, I could justify dismissing you because you are very disruptive. However, I believe deep down you're the same girl I was years back. As hard as you try to push everyone away, you just wanna be embraced by them. In order for that to happen, you gotta change."

It was hard hearing the words she was saying to me. One thing I did know was that she cared. Maybe I needed to take a look at what she said. I felt like life had dealt me an unfair hand. She was telling me to play that hand, and maybe

I'd see that I could win. Either way, it was my move. What was I gonna do?

"I made you dinner tonight, baby. Let me come scoop you up," Rico said to me the next night.

I had a project due for English. With all the extra practice we had been doing in cheerleading, I did not have time to play. He begged and pleaded and told me again that he had cooked for me. He wanted me to see his campus apartment. So I said yes.

Fast as he could, he said, "Cool, I'm on my way out."

This was going to be my first real date with Rico. I went and took a quick shower. I put on my best undergarments; not because he was going to get lucky, but because I wanted to feel sexy. It had been twenty-four hours since all the drama in the locker room. Once again Ella and I shared the same space, but no words were spoken. However, I needed a favor from her, so I had to be the bigger person.

"Ah, could you please tell Mom I went out?" I asked as nicely as I could, being vague on purpose.

"Where you going? It's almost ten. You probably need to run that by Mom first."

"Like I can call her on her job," I responded, knowing our mom did not like us bothering her.

Ella retorted, "You know you can call her, Eva."

"Yeah, for emergencies."

"You need to stay in without her permission. Besides, Eva, anybody who goes out after nine is looking for a booty call."

So ticked, I copped an attitude. "Whatever! That's not true."

"What else do you think a guy wants this time of night?"

"Not that I owe you an explanation, but he cooked me dinner. I might even be back before Mom gets off work." My sister turned her head and walked away. "If you don't wanna help me out, I can leave her a note," I said angrily.

Ella looked back at me and said, "Well, I suggest you get to writing."

At that point we hated each other. A car pulled up in our carport. I rushed outside.

"Dang, that was quick," I said to myself.

But I stopped short when I saw all the girls piling out of Charli's new black BMW. That girl wanted for nothing.

"Well, what are you all done up for, Eva?" Charli sniffed, eyeing my outfit.

"You better get your girl," I said to Hallie.

"You better slow your roll before you end up with something you'll regret," Charli retorted.

I certainly wanted them to be in the house before Rico showed up. But fate would have it otherwise.

Rico rolled down his window and talked in a sly tone. "Hey, girls, I got room for you too."

I could not get in his car fast enough. Whacking him upside his head was the first thing I did after shutting the door. Why did he front on me?

Rico cried out, "What? That hurt!"

"Why you flirting with my friends?"

"Dang, I was just teasing. I was saying I had enough."

"Enough what?"

"Food, dang. It's cool if you wanna keep me to yourself, baby." Rico stared at me. "Dang, girl, you look all pretty and smell all good."

He touched my leg. He was looking too much at me and not as much on the road. Quickly, I buckled up.

"Watch where you going," I lectured.

"Can't keep my eyes from lookin' at what you showin'. You makin' a brotha crazy."

"Well, I need you to keep a sista alive. How 'bout that? I can button up." I did.

"I like you, Eva. You so spunky. I can just only imagine."

"Only imagine then, 'cause I told you it's not going down tonight. If that's what you want, you need to take me back home."

"Why? You ain't trying to hold out on me, are you?"

"No, I'm just trying to get to know you."

"What you wanna know? I wanna be a rapper. I'm working on a record deal. I'll be shooting a music video in a couple months, and the record label been casting a bunch of these college girls, but I ain't feelin' 'em."

Something inside of me perked up. I was not trying to be a model, but I *was* gorgeous. So what if other people thought I showed it off too much? Why waste it?

"Maybe you can be in it with me. Your pretty self will sure sell some records," Rico purred. He cupped my chin in his hand.

Was he deliberately being stupid? Did he think I was naive? I was not one of those girls you could just say anything to. I needed proof. I would be so hyped to be on BET or MTV—like any other normal teenage girl—but I was not going to believe him just because.

"Yeah, right," I said, pulling up to his apartment.

I was impressed to see he had a two bedroom. One room was made into a makeshift recording studio. It was real bootleg, but it was enough for him to drop a few beats. He played me a little somethin' somethin', and I could not help but sway, rock, and move my hips to the beat.

"What's your name gonna be?" I asked.

"Well, you know there was a Rico Suave. I'm Rico Swagga."

"Hey," I said with excitement. We both started dancing.

"You mind if I get you on tape? I think if I show you to the record executives, they will love you. We wouldn't have to worry about a casting call, and you can have the part for real. It's paying a lil' somethin' too."

He showed me some papers that looked like a contract, but he would not let me read them. He said it was confidential. Though I had not heard of Slap Out Records, the paperwork looked official.

"I ain't gonna beg you to be in the video. It's your call," Rico said. He started to set up the camera.

"No, no, I wanna do it. It's just that I'm hungry, that's all."

No wonder I didn't see a bunch of pots and pans in the kitchen. He only had hot dogs on the stove. What spread?

"I thought you said you fixed me a meal."

"What? A brotha ain't no chef. I did cook for you."

Rico did not even give my food time to digest. Before I knew it, he had me standing up. He turned his music back on and turned on the camera. He wanted to see me work my moves.

"Nah, you too stiff. I saw you dance at the party. Don't hold back."

Trying to feel it, I said, "Perform for me.

Maybe that will loosen me up."

"Oh, you ain't said nothing but a word."

When he said the lyrics, I was appalled. There was so much profanity and negative talk about women. I could not imagine what my friends and family would say if they saw me in a video dancing to these words.

"This is not for me," I declared. I frowned and moved away.

Quickly, he said, "Wait, that's not the track we'd be using for the dancing. I just thought you wanted me to lighten the mood." Then he started singing, "I wanna get wit my girl for the first time. I wanna have the feeling that she's all mine. I want our bodies to collide on the dance floor. And shake it, take it to the bedroom for lots more. 'Cause when she gets to know all of me, there's no other place she'd rather be. Let's hit it, hit it for the first time."

As he started singing, he started taking off his shirt. Then he came over to me and start saying over and over again how beautiful I was. He went to the kitchen and came back with some wine coolers. I could tell as he lit the candle that he wanted to make the song he just sang our reality.

"You know what? I think its time for me to go now."

"You have not finished the dancing session," he commanded. Then he went over to the camera and appeared to turn it off.

"I don't think being in a video is for me."

"That's cool. Won't pressure you with dat. Why don't you just ease up some? Take a lil' sip; have a lil' nip."

"I don't want anything to drink."

"Aight, I'll take you home. Can I at least have a hug though? A kiss? Something?"

I went over to him. Instead of just a little peck I planned on giving him, he made sure his tongue slid way down my throat. He was grabbing me firmly, but I pulled back.

"Stop, I just wanted to spend time with you. I just wanted to get to know you. I just wanted to kick it for a bit."

"What? You trying to fall in love and stuff? I ain't one of them lil' high school boys at Lockwood. I'm looking for a big girl, and I thought that's what you were. You coming over to my place at ten o'clock at night, and you just wanna talk. Wassup? Let me rub on them thighs."

"You wanna rub my thigh, that's all?" I said, feeling like if I just let him do that, he would have had enough for a minute.

He smiled when I walked to him. "That's it, come here. Smile for me. That's right. Relax, baby, relax."

CHAPTER 3
Have Discretion

Relax? I am relaxed," I said to Rico. I tried to shove him away.

He pulled me back real quick. Rico started biting my neck. He got rough quickly.

"Ow," I cried.

"Come on, please," Rico said, using his hands to keep me close. "As much sass as you got, I know you like it rough."

"Like *what* rough?"

Rico shoved me down on his couch. "Quit moving around, dang. You know you want this."

He ripped open my shirt. He tore off my bra. When I tried to kick him, he punched me in the arm.

"Look, I'm not gonna fight you for what I know you want. I bring you to my place, try to make you a star, treat you all special, and you gonna give me a hard time. I thought you liked it rough, but not this rough."

As he continued having his way with me, everything became a haze. I did remember saying no repeatedly. But I was ignored. He thought only of himself, violating every part of my being.

As tears rolled down my face, I thought about my life. What had I done to deserve this? Why was he taking what I said he could not have? How come what was supposed to feel so good was so painful?

When he was done, I wanted to kill him. But I did not have a gun. I was sure he had a knife somewhere, however, so I rushed into the kitchen when he went to the bathroom. I started fumbling through drawers. I forgot about the knife when I saw a washcloth. Immediately, I turned on the faucet, not caring what temperature the water was. I started washing every inch that he touched until I realized I was in pain from the scalding water, from the assault, and from my aching soul.

"Dang, baby, I was gonna let you go in the bathroom when I was done," he noted, coming over to me and trying to kiss me.

I could not speak. I tried to say, "You bastard! I hate you. You better sleep with one eye open mother ... ugh."

I was just so overwhelmed. I could not say anything. I wanted to tell him off, but there he stood trying to cuddle me, like this was all good. Like he had given me something I wanted. Like he was my doggone boyfriend.

To make the night even stranger, his phone rang. He picked it up quickly. Then he started yelling into the receiver.

He screamed, "I told you we can't get together until one. Yes, I have someone else over here with me, like I owe your dumb self an explanation. You just be ready when I come and get you."

I looked at him with a blank stare. It all made so much sense now. You could not just go out with guys who looked all good, smelled all nice, and said the right words. Heck no. You had to know them. You had to tell someone where you were going. You had to be smart about what time you went out in the first place. My sister turned out to be right. When you went out with a guy after a certain time, chances were it was a booty call. Unfortunately, I learned the hard way that when you resist your date, you have already given him access, and when you deny him, he will stop at nothing to satisfy himself.

He saw me looking and said, "What's the problem, baby? That wasn't anybody on the phone. We just got to do a little studying, that's all. So let me get you on home so your mom don't call the police. Plus, I need to get back and get some schoolwork done. You said you had a project too, right?"

Rico was crazy, and I had no one to blame but myself. Thankfully, on the car ride home he was on his cell phone. He thought I was asleep, but my eyes were just swollen from crying. He was bragging to some guy, and I caught the jerk in a lie.

"Yeah, she bought the record-label trick. You know, you got to print me out another contract. I spilled something on this one I got. Yeah, it was good. High school meat is always fresh. Even the ones that look like they stink."

It was interesting because at that moment, when I thought I had nothing left that he could take, he grabbed the last ounce of dignity I had left when he shared with his homeboy or whoever he was talking to that basically he thought I was trash. When we pulled up to my house, he did not have to touch me, try to wake me, or tell me to get out. I opened the door, slammed it on him, and never looked back.

Charli's car was still in the carport. The girls were all working on a presentation with Ella and had gotten permission from their parents to stay late. I had to walk past them to get to the bedroom. I needed to grab my pajamas and get in the shower. My hair was mangled, my clothes were ripped, and I looked like the tramp of the night. For the first time, everything they were thinking about me I felt about myself. Coach Woods tried to tell me to slow my roll, but I would not listen. Now I was shattered. I was unable and unwilling to carry on.

"You can't say hi?" Charli called out.

Randal, having my back, said, "Leave her alone. Can't you see she's tired?"

Charli grunted. I could not be mad at her. Actually, I could not hate that Charli, Ella, and Randal were saving themselves.

While Hallie was not pure, she was not stained like me. She realized she wanted self-respect. She did not put herself out there with any Tom, Dick, or Rico. I was the only idiot of our bunch. Finally, it was like I had on glasses and could see what I had been doing to myself. For so long, I thought it was them. Them missing out on life. Them not letting their womanhood shine. Them not knowing how to truly work men with the power of seduction. Well, the joke was on me.

The shower could not get hot enough. The brand new bar of soap, which I just opened, was not big enough. My washcloth was not wide enough to help me erase it all.

There was a knock on the bathroom door. I said nothing. The knock intensified.

"Eva, it's Randal. Eva, you've been in that bathroom for a long time. Eva? Are you all right?"

"Go away," I shouted, sitting at the bottom of the tub in a fetal position while the water sprayed down on me.

"I just want to make sure you're okay, that's all," she whispered.

"It's late, Randal, please. Please, y'all go."

"We're done. We're leaving."

Then she was gone. I was relieved. I could not even muster up the strength to say thanks.

A few moments later, my sister was pounding on the door. "Eva, I need to get in there. You know this isn't fair. You've been in there for who knows how long. There won't be any hot water left for me."

I wanted to call out, "Help me, Ella! Hold me, Ella! Protect me, sis." However, all I could do was find the strength to turn off the water, dry myself off, brush my teeth, and crawl into bed. I could not let my sister know what I had done to myself. I could not tell her that she had me pegged all along.

"Why are you making all that noise, Eva? You're keeping me awake. Are you talking in your sleep over there?" Ella questioned.

The noise she heard was me crying. I could not hold back the tears. I could not close my eyes without seeing the image of Rico. Except in my thoughts, he looked different. His hands were like claws, his face was like the Incredible Hulk, and his body was hairy like a werewolf. I was distraught and destroyed.

I heard the knob turn on our bedroom door, and my mom flicked on the lights. After grumbling to herself she said, "Okay, girls, what in the world is going on in here? I come home after working all day and I'm tired. I don't feel like having to play referee between the two of you guys."

Normally, I would have defended myself and said, "Do you hear me saying anything? Although our voices sound alike to most, you know the difference, Mom. Come on, that was Ella. Get off my back."

This was not a normal circumstance. I just took it. I actually think that surprised both of them. They got wide-eyed and looked my way.

My mom said, "Eva, look at me. I know you're not asleep. I heard the two of you guys fussing."

"It was only me talking," Ella confessed.

There was my sister again, proving to be an abnormal person. She wouldn't throw me under the bus if she could take all the blame herself. And she *always* took the blame herself. When we were little, if she broke a jar, then she'd admit it. If she drank out of the milk carton, she admitted it. Every time she was caught, she did not get in trouble because our mom could not get angry with her sweet child.

I should have learned a long time ago, being honest is better than fabricating some lie. When I broke the window, I would say I did not know who did it. I got a spanking when I ate all the leftovers and did not leave Ella any. I told my mom it was friends who were over, but when I got sick from gorging on the sweet potato pie, my mom said that I got what I deserved. When I applied pressure on my sister to do something bad, I told my mom she wanted to do it, but she never believed me, and I got punished.

Yeah, I should have learned a long time ago that honesty was the only way to go. I needed my mom and sister to love me. I needed them both to embrace me. I needed them both to quit all the fussing and be there for me. I had gotten myself into some serious trouble, and the hell hole I was in, in my mind, was unbearable.

Ella said, "I was going off because she just gets on my nerves, Mom, okay?"

"Well, I need the two of you guys to fix it. I'm serious. I don't care if you have to stay up all night and still go to school in the morning.

Handle it. Y'all know I don't play that. I work too hard around here for y'all to treat each other any kind of way. Sisters, identical twins, are supposed to get along. Fix it!" she hollered before slamming the door.

"It's just not that easy," I surprised myself and muttered under my breath.

"I'm sure it's not that easy for you to tell me why you thought it was okay to show your private parts to my boyfriend. I know he's not a doggone virgin, but still, when it comes to seeing me—*us*—our identical parts—now all that's gone because you showed him. I just don't understand why you'd even do it."

She just kept going off on me, and rightfully so. I was wrong. However, I could not take it.

Very emotional, I screamed back, "I'm sorry! I was stupid, okay? Your sister is a slut. There! He still likes you, doesn't he? At least he respects you. At least he's willing to wait until you're ready. At least he didn't just take it from you."

"What? What are you saying? What are you talking about?" Ella rushed over to my bed. She stroked my forehead.

I moved to the corner of my bed. I did not want her touching me. I thought I wanted her to hold me, but I could not take it.

"Eva, please talk to me. Please tell me what's going on. Don't shut me out. Are you saying that college guy ..."

I rolled over at her empathy and nodded.

"No, Eva, no. We gotta go tell Mom," she declared, getting up.

I quickly grabbed her hand and pulled her back down. "Please, no. Nobody can know. I did this to myself."

"You didn't do anything to yourself. I know you're not trying to take the blame for this. If he raped you, then that's his fault, and he should go to jail. You can't keep quiet."

"You don't know!" I finally said. "Who's gonna believe me? All you guys thought, when y'all looked at me when I came in here, that I was nothing. You even said before I left, if you leave late at night going to a guy's house, he wants one thing. I walked around with skimpy clothes thinking I looked cute and guys just saw past the fabric. I don't know if Randal told you, but the reason I cut up with Leo is because I heard you guys talking about me. The sad part about it is y'all were right. Who would want to be like me? Who would want to end up like this? Who would want to be so broken?"

"Oh, Eva," Ella said. "I'm so sorry. I'm sorry he hurt you. You can't deal with this alone. That guy was wrong. You were always able to say stop. Student council has been passing pamphlets out about this. There will be an assembly about this topic soon. I didn't know what you were saying over there, and I'm sorry ... I ... Uh ... I just need you to talk to Mom. Please don't make me keep this secret."

"You know our pact," I said. "When one of us comes to the other with something serious, we agreed we would keep the confidence. I need you to promise me you will do that. I'm breaking here, Ella, worse than I ever have before."

My sister tried holding me, but I did not let her. She tried again and I jerked away. She tried one more time, and I fell into her arms.

I just kept saying, "Don't tell, please, don't tell. Please, don't say anything, please."

She kissed my forehead, wiped away my tears, and said she would not. I might not have had the help I needed, but I surely had my sister's love. For now, at least I had a little more peace.

The next morning I woke up extra early. I had my mom take me to school before my sister rose. While I still needed to work on my project, I did not want to have to look at my sister, knowing she knew everything.

"You're mighty quiet this morning. You and Ella work things out?" my mom asked.

"Yes, ma'am," I responded.

"Yes, ma'am? Since when did you become so proper? Eva, talk to me. What's wrong?"

"Nothing. I'm okay," I said, trying to hold it together because I did not want to break down.

"I know it's been rough on you, me calling you out in front of the principal and all. Eva, the man could have suspended you. Besides, I don't want you to turn this all around and get mad at me and stay over there and say nothing. You know I like conversation on the ride, and you brought the tongue lashing out on yourself."

I looked down at my hands. I had acrylic nails, and two of them had broken off pretty bad. That must have happened in the struggle. One of them was so jagged it was dangerous, and if Rico were standing in front of me, I would use it to tear him up.

"I mean, Eva, as much as I'd like to think the world is fair, it's not. Women who have a reputation of being too loose have it harder in the respectable world. Do you understand what I'm saying, honey? You're just sitting over there."

I nodded. That was all I could do. I had no get up and go. My spunk was gone, and whether anyone liked it or not, I was a different person.

While in school, I was in a daze. I did not even perk up in the substitute's class. Mr. Gunn seemed nice. All the girls were making goo-goo eyes, but I was not in that number. Randal sat next to me. She kept looking my way, wondering why I had not commented on the man in charge of giving us math instruction.

When you are going through drama, you see the world from a different point of view. I could tell that Randal was sad. I called her out about not defending me. However, now my brash tactics needed to be recanted. I was too ashamed to even open my mouth. I tried as best as I could to smile her way so that she could feel better.

I was also sensitive to the girls who were not as popular, like the chick with glasses and braces who dressed like someone from forty years ago. While she seemed oblivious to the fact that her style was off, she had a melancholy air about her that longed to want to fit in.

Inwardly, I shouted, "Stay the way you are, girl. Cover up and be careful. Be happy you're in your glasses and braces. Don't flaunt too early, because if you do, you'll run the risk of getting your innocence stolen."

Time seemed to drag. I hated that I had to stay after school for cheerleading practice. I did not want to dress out; I was afraid people would see the bruises. Also, I did not want to take my clothes off. Psychologically, I was all messed up, so I asked Coach if I could sit out.

"What's wrong?" she wondered.

"Just girl stuff, Coach."

"You want to lie down in my office?"

"That would be great if you don't mind."

She looked at me as if she knew there was something else I wanted to say. My eyes were crying out for help. I did not know if she could tell that or not.

"You need an aspirin? Want me to get you some water, anything?"

I shook my head. Before she left, I got the strength to say, "You were right about everything else, Coach. I don't want you to think I didn't hear."

She came back in and said, "Oh, Eva, I've been a little on edge ever since we had that talk. I was hoping you took it the right way. I just want to help you. You've got so much potential, and I hate for unwise choices to bring harm to you, you know?"

I knew. I could not let her know how I knew, but I knew.

"Get some rest and come on out to practice when you feel better."

"Yes, ma'am," I murmured. Coach did a double take, stunned at my politeness.

What kind of person had I been? How brash and disrespectful had I been? While I felt that I could never get over what happened to me, it was also painful coming to grips with the fact that some of what I endured was actually making me better. The problem was that I was still broken.

Charli and Hallie came in Coach's office during the break. Charli said, "Look, Randal told us that you overheard us talking about you."

"She's got a big mouth," I uttered.

"And truth be told, you got a big, nasty reputation."

"That's what I'm hearing," I retorted. I really needed the two of them to leave.

I was in no mood for their lecture. What they were saying to me was not half as tough as what I was saying to myself. At least I knew my love for myself was real. I was really truly beginning to question theirs.

"Hallie, do you have anything to say to me?" I uttered. "Or do you just follow along with everything she says?"

Hallie said, "Yeah, I know people talked about me last year too, but for the record, I was never in front of the school having sex."

"Believe everything you hear and spread it around, huh?" I glared at my old buddy.

"Well, if you didn't walk around here looking like you want to gobble up every man in sight, then I wouldn't believe any ol' thing. When it barks like a dog, it ain't a fish," Hallie replied, trying to get backbone.

I did not know what Hallie was talking about, and I really did not care. "Can y'all just get out?" I begged, wanting space.

"Listen, Coach said you weren't feeling well," Charli stepped in and brashly said. "And as captain, I need you out there. So if there's any way you can save the drama for another time and get on out there so we can practice, it would be much appreciated."

"No," I snapped. I did not appreciate her tone.

Charli huffed, "No? What's wrong with you?"

"What are y'all doing here?" Ella came in and asked.

Charli explained, "Trying to get your sister to quit tripping and come on to practice. She told Coach Woods that she was tired and sick. Look at her. There's nothing wrong, and she's in no pain. She's just being lazy."

"You don't even know what you're talking about, Charli, okay?" Ella defended. "You need to get out of Eva's face, back off, and take her for her word."

"What? Don't play, Ella," Charli said.

"Do I look like I'm playing? She doesn't feel well. Leave her the heck alone. I know you're the captain, but you need to know how to motivate people the right way and not alienate them."

Charli responded, "This is already hard enough to do because we don't have you for the routine because of your injury."

"Well, Charli, it's not like Ella can help it," Hallie spoke up. "She got shot."

"Shut up, Hallie," Charli snapped.

"Wait, shut up? Who you telling to shut up?" Ella said. Then she got in Charli's face.

Charli stepped back. "Let's not turn this around. Let's not twist this around. Don't get mad at me because she's sitting over there acting like something is wrong. Ain't nothing wrong with her tail. If a guy walked in here right now, she'd get up, prance in his face, and try to get him to notice her. I'm sick of Eva thinking she's all that."

I wanted to stand to my feet, break up the tension, and just scream out loud, "No, something truly *is* wrong with me, Charli. Because I was too wild, I did learn a lesson."

But I felt too ashamed to say a word. Too beaten down to make a case for myself. No one needed to know what happened to me but my sister. I had to keep my mouth closed and have discretion.

CHAPTER 4

Inconceivable Finish

I can't believe you talked me into doing this," I said to Ella. We were junior bridesmaids, for my dad and Samantha's wedding.

Over the last couple of days, since Ella stood up to Charli for me, I had been able to appreciate my sister more. I was able to open up to her and enjoy a bond that my mom always wanted us to have. She showed me she cared and was not my enemy. I liked her covering me. She was tougher than I thought.

Standing in Lakeside Baptist Church's more private sanctuary and not the big one that held three thousand people on Sunday, I knew I had to be honest. I wanted my parents back together. Since that was not happening and my dad really cared about me being involved, I had to stop being selfish. I had to help bring to life the desires of others who I cared for.

I wondered if my dad even knew the minister who was performing the ceremony. Pastor Lawrence King was almost like a god around these parts. Turn on any Christian channel and you would see him there. When you needed him to do pastor things, he was absent.

Landon King was one of the football players I was cool with. He was Pastor King's son, and everyone knew he resented his father. In a time like this, I resented Pastor Bigwig too. My dad paid a lot of tithes and was a faithful member. It was bad that when you gave so much to build the church, the pastor could not be there to help in your time of need. Guess you had the option of going to a smaller church.

I looked over at my dad; he seemed out of it. Maybe my dad was worried that his bride would drop her baby any minute. Maybe he just wasn't sure that this was the right move because he certainly was nervous. I wanted to go tug on him and say, "Hey, we can bounce. All you got to do is say the word." However, every time I mumbled, my sister hit my leg.

"Hush," Ella instructed.

"Whatever! You can stand here and look all excited, but not me," I grunted.

There were about fifty people in attendance. A bunch of my family I didn't know and family of Miss Samantha's. Boy, she got under my skin like a bad rash. Regardless of my feelings, they tied the knot.

They had a reception in one of the halls at the church after the ceremony. My mom was not there. I couldn't wait to get home and hug her. I wasn't sure she was over my dad. My parents were never married, and I was fairly certain that tying the knot was something my mom still longed for. Besides, before we left the house, she said we were beautiful, but she was not smiling when she said it.

"You okay?" my sister asked when she came back to her seat after visiting our relatives. "We got our great uncle here and some cousins. Get up and meet people, Eva."

But I didn't want to meet anybody. So what that we had relatives there? I was practically grown, and now was not a time to meet folks on my dad's side of the family. It was really sort of insulting. If they cared enough to want to meet me, where had they been all my life? I watched them with Evan, my dad's little boy. And *he* knew everybody.

Unable to stand all the happiness, I rushed to the bathroom. I didn't want to be anywhere near the bride, so I wanted to walk out when I saw her in there primping.

"Well, if it isn't Miss Eva," she taunted. In that instant she verified that all bygones were not bygones. She and I still had a fire. "I was so surprised you stood up for me at my wedding," my dad's new wife sneered.

"I stood up for my dad," I said, adding fuel.

"Ha-ha, yes, your dad. When you left my house quoting things that were in a personal text conversation between your father and me, I went and pulled his phone. I found it mysterious that I could not find the thread of communication between the two of us that I felt was out of character for him."

My eyes looked everywhere but at her. She had won. She had married my dad. Where was she going with this?

"I just came in here to use the restroom," I responded. I tried to push past her.

"No, we need to get a few things straight right now, missy."

"Missy? Who you talking to, Samantha?"

"I'm talking to you. Your dad wanted me to let it go and wanted you to stand up for us thinking that magically it was gonna make you all excited about me. Until I get you straight, you know you can't just pull any old thing on me. I come to you straight up with street talk. That's the only way I'ma get your respect."

"My *respect*? Please!" I snapped, fanning the flames between us. "So you went to my dad and asked him about the texts, and he said what? He had no idea. Why would he admit that he typed that to you?"

"Your dad would never lie to me," she responded quickly.

"Okay, so if you think I did it, why are you bringing it up to me? Perhaps it's because I wasn't the only one who saw him standing at the alter messing with his collar, like he was being choked standing there with you or something."

"What are you talking about?"

"If you checked his collar now, you will see it's loose and all wet. He was sweating profusely, probably wishing he could back out."

"He's never gonna run out on me and our children. He *married* me. He didn't shack up like he did with your mom."

If she wasn't pregnant, I swear I would have knocked her out even though I was in a holy building. Samantha did not have to go there. This was between us. My mom did not need to be dragged into it.

"When a man doesn't want to be tied down, eventually, he finds a way to undo the rope. I give him six months," I said, passing the rash on to her.

"Ugh, you make me sick," she hissed.

"Why? Because I got you figured out?" I yelled. "You're the kind of woman who's there for my dad because he has something. Let all his clients get up and walk out. He brings in no income. Would you stand by his side if he was broke? I didn't hear for better or worse in your vows. I'm only seventeen, but I know when people don't wanna say the traditional stuff it's because they've already got doubt."

"What are you talking about? Your father and I don't have any doubts."

"Nah, Evan is three, and you're about to have another baby. It's taken him, what? Four years to marry you. He wasn't dragging his feet. Except I thought the marriage came before the babies. Looks like you're not that much different from my mom after all. Like I said, I give it six months. Nah, the way my dad looked like he didn't wanna be there, I'll give it three—"

Samantha cut me off and gripped my arm. "I don't feel good."

"I'm sure you don't feel good," I sneered. I pulled away, wanting her to let go of my arm.

She clutched her stomach like a woman about to be robbed holds on to her purse. Then she grabbed the sink with both her hands. She started rocking side to side.

Fed up with her, I said, "Please, quit acting, Samantha."

"I don't feel good, okay? You're just evil. This is my wedding day. I'm standing here nine months pregnant, and you're stressing me out."

"I'm stressing *you* out? I just came in the bathroom to empty my bladder. You're the one who got all up in my face, and now you wanna talk about wanting peace and stuff."

"I am having the baby now."

"Samantha, please."

She tightened her grasp on the sink. She leaned over it like she wanted to throw up except nothing came out her mouth. A gush of something hit the floor, like someone smashed a punch bowl.

"My water just broke! I'm in labor. Go get your dad, please. Now, Eva, please!"

I ran out the bathroom and screamed, "Dad, Ella, somebody come quick. Call nine-one-one! She's having a baby!"

My father rushed into the bathroom. "Thank you, Eva. So glad that she was not in here by herself."

"Please, don't thank her. Help me! It's her fault." Samantha shot daggers of hate my way that burned my soul.

My dad looked up at me with a face that was so hurt and confused. I stepped out of the bathroom, ran down the church hall, and bumped into Landon King. He and I both looked like our worlds were shattered. There was no way his could be worse than mine. Now my dad was going to hate me. I was in a church, yet it felt like I was in hell.

Later that evening, we were at Lockwood. We were having a Saturday night football game. We were playing Langston Hughes High of Fulton County, and it was anyone's guess who was going to win.

"You okay?" Ella asked. We walked to the sidelines to get ready to cheer.

Usually we had to be there really early, but my mom talked to Coach Woods and explained we were coming from my dad's wedding. My sister looked at me, wanting an answer; in fact she knew I was not okay. She was the only one, other than Rico, who knew what I had been through. Add to that the drama with my dad and his new bride. My life was a mess. How could I be okay? Now wasn't the time or place to talk about it. I just had to get through the game and figure life out. I was tired of unraveling like a spool of thread.

It was a tight game. Defense on both sides of the ball was playing hard. While I was there,

I really did not want to be there. However, I was such a tough girl that I had to get a hold of myself. Being at a football game was not helping. There was too much noise, making my eardrums hurt. There were too many people looking at me and making me feel uncomfortable. There was too much of a responsibility as a cheerleader to smile. Smiling was the last thing I wanted to do.

The score was 14–0 at halftime. Unless we scored, our undefeated record would be gone. Blake's passes were bombs. Was he throwing to us cheerleaders? That's how far off his passes were. Then he threw the ball in Landon's direction. It was not a pretty pass either. It almost touched the ground, except Landon extended his left arm, juggled the ball, reeled it in, secured it, rolled, was not touched, got up, and ran it for a touchdown.

I was such a sports fanatic. However, everyone was screaming but me. Don't get me wrong, I was happy for our team and particularly happy for Landon. Again, I had seen and heard a few things that were tough in his life. I really wasn't paying attention to any rumors, but I knew he needed to smile.

Our guys had really come through. They scored two more touchdowns in the second half and kept our undefeated record intact. I was glad the game was over so I could go home. I couldn't jog off the field fast enough. Surprisingly, my dad was there.

"I thought Mom was coming to pick us up," I said to him.

"She is."

"Why aren't you at the hospital? The baby's okay and everything, right?"

"Thankfully, my baby's fine, but no thanks to you," he snarled like a grizzly bear at me.

"Dad, just hear me out."

"No, you need to hear *me* out, Eva. Samantha told me everything that was going on. I didn't mention anything to you about the texts. You're a teenager, and I get that I let you down in life, so I was going to look past that. But telling her I wasn't ready to get married and that our marriage would be over soon has to be dealt with. You had no right to do that, Eva. I can't believe you would say something like that. You put pressure on my wife. That was low. I just came here to tell you that you need to respect my marriage. You got that? Do you understand me?"

"If you wanna get mad at me, Dad, because I called it like I saw it, fine. If you're gonna give a reason as to why we're not gonna be cool like we haven't been for I don't know how many years, I'm down with that. I get it, but do not make me feel like all of this is my fault. If I don't know how to love, if I've been hard on people, if my tactics are too brash in life, look in the mirror!" I gave him a long, angry stare, turned, and stormed off.

That's what I get. I opened my heart to my dad, and he just took a hammer and pounded on it. I just felt like blood was gushing from my life. There was no way I could stop the bleeding.

I went into the bathroom to get some tissues. My dad wasn't the only one who needed to look in the mirror. I did have to take ownership of my own actions. I could blame him for this. I could blame him for that. But I was almost eighteen. I texted my mom to see if she was in the parking lot. I was so happy to see her text back that she was. I knew I needed to go find my sister to see if she was going home or if she was gonna hang with her friends. But as soon as I stepped out of the girls bathroom, I was met with another surprise.

"Hey, gorgeous. I couldn't wait to get to this game tonight so I could get with ya and have more fun," slimy and sleazy Rico oozed.

I couldn't believe Rico was standing in front of me. I wanted to take both of my hands, wrap them around his neck, and choke him. He needed to be gone.

"Please, get out of my way," I yelled.

He stepped in front of me and blocked my way. "Wassup? Why you tryna get away? Let's talk, baby. You know you wanna have some more fun with me."

"I don't ever wanna 'be with you' again. I said no and you took it."

"Ha, I know you ain't saying I raped you," he declared. "Girl, please, you came over to my house practically begging me."

"That's not true! Don't you lie! Don't you lie!" I screamed.

"You need to calm down. I don't want nobody thinking that I'ma monster."

"Leave me alone, Rico. Get out of my face. I'm tryna get away."

"Get away? Like I'ma hurt you? Oh, see, we need to talk about this."

"My mom is waiting for me. Don't make me scream. You see those security guards over there? I will scream." He stepped to me real close, put his hand on my shoulder, and squeezed down hard enough to make me wince.

"Let me make sure I'm really clear with you. Get this, Eva, you don't wanna mess with me. I will take you down. Right now, you need to recant this whole stupid accusation that I took it."

"I'm not taking anything back. That's what happened," I defended, not believing his threat.

"Oh, you're gonna regret that," he threatened. Like what else could he do to me?

"Are you threatening me?" I said to him, knowing he'd already taken all I had.

"Are you taking back what you said?"

"*No!*" I shoved him and ran.

I knew that he was acting weird the night we were together, like everything was great. Like that's what I wanted. Seriously, really, truthfully, did he think it was all cool? I could not believe he thought that. And to make it worse, he thought I wanted *more* foolishness. Was he crazy? Was I gonna let him get away with this? This was too much. Maybe Ella was right and I needed to tell somebody. Keeping this to myself was killing me, and I wanted to live.

All the boys were looking at cell phones, laughing, smiling, and kidding around. When I approached the bunch, guys started hitting each other. Some were looking at me strangely.

Ignoring them, I walked up to Ella and said, "Mom's out here; I really need to go."

"Why are you shaking?" she asked.

"It's that guy, Rico. He's here. He just threatened me."

"What?"

"Don't know why you two are all mad at *us*." Charli was back. She came over to Ella and me. "If the shoe fits, wear it," Charli added rudely.

"Huh? Just step away, Charli. We're dealing with something right now," I said.

"Oh yeah, you're dealing with something. I can't believe you're showing your face around here," Charli looked in my eyes and said.

"Just leave it alone," Hallie said to her. "Something's not right with this stuff."

"It's bad, Eva," Randal commented.

At that moment, I looked at my sister. I knew it was bad that I had been raped, but why shouldn't I show my face? I didn't do anything wrong. What was Charli talking about? What had my sister told them? I was already frazzled; now, I had to deal with cheer drama. I took my sister by the hand and pulled her over to the side. I threw my hands in the air. I needed an explanation. My stance was demanding, but she looked at me dumbfounded.

"What are you looking at me weird for?" Ella asked.

"Looking at you? Please. Why are all these people looking at me? What did you tell?"

"I promise, I didn't say nothing to nobody," she answered.

"Did you say something to somebody?" I asked, thinking it might have slipped to her boyfriend and he told folks.

Just as I thought of Leo, he came out of the locker room looking for his girl. Obviously, he thought I was bullying her because he bulldozed his way between us like I was someone he needed to tackle. I knew he was already upset with me because of the weird predicament I put him in during the locker room incident. However, he didn't have to be cruel.

"Why you all up in her face, Eva? If you wanna put yourself out there, and you think that's cute and fine, that's great. But don't you know that Ella gets affected by the things you do. You guys are twins. People fretting on me like it's my girl out there like that."

"Why people fretting on you?" Ella asked. "Its okay. We are just having a little misunderstanding."

"No, I'm sick and tired of everything always being about Eva. You've got feelings in this whole thing," Leo fumed. "This is way over-the-top this time. It's not funny, and everybody on the team is laughing about it."

"See, Ella, everybody knows. Why did you tell him?" I asked my sister.

"What do you mean, why did she tell? It's out for the world to see," Charli butted in. She handed us Blake's cell phone. "Nobody said anything. This just started floating around."

"What's been floating around?" I asked.

Charli said, "Look, it's in your hand."

I looked down at the iPhone and opened up a text message that read, "Check out the biggest slut of the school." I could not believe what I was watching. There were no words, but there was a video of me dancing. Then it cut to me being forced onto the couch. The guy's back was turned the whole time, and it was just as violent looking at it as it was experiencing it.

At the end of the clip, there was a blank black screen with white words that read, "Some like it rough." I could not believe what I was reading. I could not believe what I was seeing. I could not believe what they were laughing about. All this had to do with me. Rico was serious when he threatened me. Just that quickly, he had sent some made-up video to my friends.

I wanted to pass out. I wanted to disappear. I wanted to be anywhere but in front of my peers. Why was this happening to me? Why was my life so upside down? Why were things so wrong?

"What is it?" Ella said softly.

I just handed her the phone. I started running, but I stumbled and fell. When I looked up, a bunch of football players were laughing at me. The receiver who won the game helped me up.

Landon said, "Y'all need to quit that, dang."

"No need to defend me, Landon, 'cause if you haven't seen it, you're missing a great show," I said sarcastically.

"I ain't even opened that text. What you do is your business."

I just looked at him and said, "Right."

Well, I appreciated that he was trying to make sure I had some dignity left. However, he was already making an assumption that everything he heard was accurate. I was so frustrated.

When I pushed Landon out of the way, he said, "What did I say?"

"Sit down and look at it."

I just kept on going and ran smack back into Rico. "You'll think twice next time you wanna cross me," he taunted.

"Why don't you just take a gun and shoot me? Don't graze my arm; you might as well aim for my heart."

"Your tough self, please, don't even act like this is fazing you. You're probably loving the attention. You think you're popular anyway. I just set it so every guy in this school wanna have a lil' taste like I did."

I reached my hand up to smack him, but he grabbed hard around my wrist.

"Let my daughter go!" my mom screamed.

Rico looked at her and jetted away. I fell into her arms. My heart was too weak to act strong.

"Mom, take me home."

"What is going on, Eva?"

"I don't wanna talk about it, Mom. I can't talk about it."

"You were upset when I picked you up from your dad's wedding. You're upset when I'm picking you up from a football game. Child, you are gonna have to talk to me. What is the problem?"

"I was raped, Mom, okay? There, you know it! You happy now?"

"What?!" she cried with appalled emotion. "Where? When? Who? I know I been working a lot. All I was trying to do was get you girls graduated from high school. Is it somebody we know? Do we need to go to the police? Did it happen after the game? What do we do next?"

"It wasn't today, okay? It was earlier in the week."

"Oh, baby, I'm so sorry." She wrapped her arms around me and held me tight.

People were walking by. Some were pointing and laughing.

"Can we please go home? *Please*."

"Where's Ella?"

"She's with Hallie."

"So all these people know?" my mom asked. More folks looked my way, scrutinizing me.

"The guy made some kind of recording."

"*What?* That's a crime."

"Mama, it's floating all around."

"No, seriously, that's legally wrong. That's called sexting. It's a criminal offense to send or forward things like that."

"I just want this to go away."

"If he's playing dirty like that, then he needs to go away," my mom uttered.

"Was that the guy who was just gripping your arm?" she asked. I nodded. "What grade is he in? He looks too old to be in school here."

"He's in college."

"Well, how did all this happen?"

"I went out with him when you were at work," I said quietly.

"Eva!"

"I know, Mom, I'm sorry. If you only knew how sorry I was. Every day I can't even breathe thinking about what happened. I can't get past it, and now this whole week has been the worst of my life," I sobbed. "I just wanna wake up from this nightmare and pretend it never happened, but my life keeps getting worse and worse and worse. I deserve this horrific week with an inconceivable finish."

CHAPTER 5
Very Broken

Curled up in a ball, sobbing uncontrollably, and wishing I was never born was my fate. I was okay when my mom got me home after the football game. Then she had to go into work for the night shift. As soon as I heard the door slam, my body broke out in hives, I got chills, and the pain became unbearable.

Why was this happening to me? When was the madness going to stop? How come my world was so upside down?

The front door opened again, and I grabbed the covers off of my bed, slid to the corner, and tried to hide. I could not explain it, but I was petrified. Was Rico coming for seconds? Did he tell some of his boys where I lived? Were guys coming because they wanted to try to carry out their own sick fantasies?

I just started screaming, "No, leave! Please, go! Don't come in. Leave now. Stop!"

Without heeding my plea, I saw a shadow come into the room, but my heart did not burst as I could see it was Ella. However, my mind would not let me truly believe and comprehend that it was her. When I saw other shadows, I really got frightened.

I screamed louder than I did at any game. "Stay away! Don't you come any closer! You guys get back! Please, get back."

My sister walked slowly to me. "Eva, it's me. It's Ella."

"Only you come, only you," I sobbed. "Tell those boys to go, please. Ella, don't let them touch me! Ella, help!"

Randal started crying and said, "Eva, it's us. We're not gonna hurt you. Please, calm down. We love you. It's Charli, Hallie, and me. That's it. No boys, I promise."

"I'm going to heat up some warm milk," Charli said. "It will soothe her."

Charli hugged Ella before exiting the room. Hallie started pacing, and Ella continued to slowly make her way over to me.

Ella wiped my tears and said lovingly, "Sis, please calm down. I know it's been a lot. I can only imagine. You can handle this; you're tough. And we're gonna help you through it."

Charli walked in with a mug. The girls were whispering. Internally, I had a war going on. Part of me said they were the enemy. A rational part said they were who they said they were and only trying to help.

When I looked up, Ella had the mug. "Here's some milk."

I just shook my head. How could I trust them? What if there was poison mixed into the cloudy white substance?

Charli came over to me and said, "You're the toughest girl I know. You might be broken, but you can be put back together stronger and better than before. Drink this milk. Come on, girl. It's us and we love you. Drink up. Trust me."

I took the cup, but my hands were shaking. After sipping a bit of the soothing drink, I could see more clearly. They were my girls. They were here to support me. They were not leaving until I was fine. And, boy, did I need them to stay.

Finally through with every drop, I sighed, feeling much better. Charli smiled, pleased with me—and herself. She took the cup from my tight grasp. I realized how much I loved Charli's bossy ways. I leaned my head forward on Charli's shoulder and sobbed worse than I ever remembered doing ever in my life.

Thirty minutes passed before I was calmer, and I crawled back into bed. There was not a dry eye in our room. All the tissue in our place was gone. My friends cared, and that moved me.

Looking up at all of them, I said, "Maybe I can get through this with you guys in my life. With y'all standing by me, maybe I'll be okay after all. Maybe I can go on and not lose it. Thanks. Thank you so much."

"You're right. You're gonna be okay," Charli declared. She rubbed my back, clearly upset and angry. "I don't know how this guy is able to walk around free. Why don't the police have him locked up?"

"I hope he didn't post bond," Hallie said in total frustration.

"Whenever they picked him up, they needed to throw away the key," Randal replied, punching her fist into her hand.

I could not look at them. They were assuming I did the right thing and reported his behind. I knew I did not. I just wanted it all to go away. Charli could pick up on my uneasy mannerisms.

As gently as she could, she asked, "Eva, please tell me you reported this."

"I ... I ...," I stuttered, but more words would not come.

"Talk to me, Eva. You of all people should not be scared," Charli grabbed my hand and demanded boldly.

"Leave her alone, Charli," Ella defended. "You guys just back up. Give her some space so she can calm down. Y'all didn't see how broke down she was after y'all left that night.

My sister pulled the three of them away from me. I could see in Charli, Hallie, and Randal's eyes that they were all dumbfounded that I kept this information to myself. I hated that I let them down. I hated even worse that I let a rapist go free. However, it wasn't as simple as they thought. My world was shattered since this happened and lucid thought was not easy to come by.

"Oh my gosh!" Randal cried out in shock. "This happened the night we were here working on the project, didn't it? No wonder you looked so disoriented, and you were in the bathroom forever."

Needing them to understand, I opened up and said, "Yeah, I was trying to scrub everything off of me. I should have, *truly should have*, gone to the police. I know it. Seeing him causing more damage makes me sick, but I just wanted this all to go away."

"The only way to make sure that this truly goes away—" Charli commented, trying to step around Ella.

Ella stood her ground. "No, Charli, you've said enough. She doesn't want to say anything. Can't you see this is hard on her?"

"It's okay," I sighed. I reached out my hand, longing for Charli's touch to give me strength.

Charli took my hand and said, "I feel for you. I hate what you're going through. I'm not trying to say it will be easy to stand up, but you have to because that guy could do this to somebody else. The problem is the video he's forwarding to people makes it look like you consented."

I shouted, "No, that's not how it happened. I thought only part of it was being taped. He told me I was auditioning for a music video. I asked for proof that he had a record deal. He showed me a contract, so I said I'd dance for the camera. Then I heard the song and wanted out. Out of dancing. Out of his place. When he came on to me, I was out of his grip. The video makes it look like I was for it, but I was saying no over and over again."

"Then let's go. Let's go to the cops right now," Charli begged, trying to get me out of bed.

Pulling my hand away, I sat flat on the bed and said, "Go to the cops? For what? Weren't you here that night? I went to the bathroom and washed away everything."

Charli continued, "Yeah, but we can testify. You came here and your clothes were torn. You appeared to be in a trance—"

"But I didn't say to any of you guys that I was raped, did I?" I explained.

Charli, being Charli said, "Cops don't care about that stuff. They wanna get the bad guys, and what this guy did to you … you got to stand."

I put my knees to my face, buried my head forward, and just started rocking again. Was Charli right? Would the police care? No way, I thought.

Venting, I looked up and uttered, "It's not gonna make a difference. It's not gonna matter. You guys—my best friends—thought I was a slut. I wasn't a virgin. I brought this on me."

"No," my sister said. "You didn't. If you said no, then he was supposed to stop. We can see that this has made you feel worthless. To help you feel strong again, we should definitely fight this and show that son of a—"

"Okay, okay," Randal said to Ella. "Let's all stay cool and not let this guy and what he did get to us. This whole thing can make us stronger."

"Yeah, let's let this make us stronger," Hallie agreed. "Eva, we are here with you and for you. You want to report this? Let's do it together."

It was 11:30 p.m. when my friends and sister wanted to take me downtown to APD to report this crime. I was angry. I was bitter. I was shattered. However, I did have a duty to at least try and protect the next girl Rico might prey upon.

So borrowing their strength that I usually never needed because I had so much of my own, I got up, put on my clothes, looked at the four of them, and said, "I'm ready."

"You sure?" Ella asked, making sure I wanted this.

"She's sure," Charli replied. She was just happy I agreed, for whatever reason.

And with that, the five of us walked out the door. Our mission was to break Rico as he had broken me. As Hallie had promised, we were on that mission together.

"Okay, this is the police station," Hallie said. We pulled up to the eerie place in downtown Atlanta in Hallie's junky car. This was no place for Charli's BMW. "This is it, Eva."

"I don't want to go in there by myself," I said to my friends.

"It's late, you guys. We should just stay together," Ella said. So we all stayed in the car as Hallie drove around back to park.

As we walked up, I got all kinds of knots and twists in my stomach, and I realized I was never going to pick on my sister again. Being the tough one for so long, I could never relate to why she got nervous or uneasy. I never felt weird, but now I clearly got it. Some things were just too much to bear, and while I had a great capacity to be able to overcome the mishaps of life, I had finally reached a breaking point.

There were two young cops at the desk. When they saw the five of us coming, they started smiling too wide. That reaction was one I usually used to my advantage. I understood that guys liked to flirt, and flirting back to get my way was my thing. Now, I was past all that. I understood that my body was more than an object. I was to be respected, appreciated, and taken seriously. It was time for business, not time for them to get their kicks. Though it was late, they were on duty, and I was not going to tolerate being mistreated.

"Well, well, well, Officer Brown, what do we have here?" the fatter guy called out to his buddy. His name badge said Officer Walker.

The taller and more underfed-looking one said, "I don't know, Officer Walker. I'd say these five pretty young ladies are probably coming in here to report their cat missing."

I could tell Charli was insulted. She rolled her eyes and looked at me like we needed to jump them. If they hadn't been cops, I would have decked them both.

Instead, the lady in her tried the sweet approach as she stepped to the two of them and said, "We need to talk to a special victims detective, and we'd appreciate professionalism."

Officer Walker was short and wide. He looked at Charli and said, "Are you insinuating—"

"I'm just saying, sir, a cat? I just told you what we're here for. This is serious. Can you get us somebody to talk to?" Charli said without flinching.

"Hold up now, missy," Officer Walker said. He shook his finger at us like we were kids. "We got to take down some information, and just because you watch *Law and Order* doesn't mean you get to come in here and try to tell us how to do our jobs."

"No, I demand to speak to your superiors so I can tell them that you are not doing your job," Charli shot back, probably wanting to tell them her dad was a state court judge, and he had friends who could get them gone.

"This wasn't a good idea," I leaned over and whispered to Ella.

Ella took her hand and bounced it up and down as if she was dribbling a basketball. "Let Charli handle it. Some guys are jerks. It's fine. This is important. We'll get to the good cops."

About ten minutes later, an older African American gentlemen came up to the front and in an irritated tone barked, "I'm Officer Crowell. Who is making the claim?"

None of us moved. The gruff officer with a belly like Santa Claus intimidated us more than the two jokers at the front desk. I sucked in my breath. There was no way, I thought, that this irritated old cop would care anything about what had happened to me.

"We all want to go back there, sir," Charli verbalized, not wanting to let me go alone.

Officer Crowell squinted and scoffed our way, clearly not liking that his question wasn't answered. "I only need to see the person making the claim. Now, unless all of you guys were violated, you'll have to remain here."

The four of them were putting up a fight with the officer. The Saint Nick impersonator was getting fed up. The front desk officers looked at him like we were a handful.

Finally, I stood up and said, "It's me. I'm the one."

"Okay, right this way." Officer Crowell exhaled. He was clearly tired of our antics.

"If you need us, you call us," Charli stressed.

"I love you," Ella said when I passed her.

"Don't hold back anything. Tell it all," Hallie advised with a supportive wink.

"I know it's hard," Randal told me. "But you can do it."

I know every officer, just like every person, has different ways. Officer Crowell was one I should be able to relate to because he was like me, straight to the point. He was not trying to make conversation. He was not trying to be my friend. He was not even trying to calm me. He just wanted facts. However, I needed compassion, and he was not the person to give it to me.

"So let me get this straight," Officer Crowell stated after hearing me explain everything. "You went over there willingly and at a late hour. You danced around in front of this video camera, but then you thought he turned it off.

You supposedly said no; however, you never came forward that night. Now that there's a recording, you're claiming that he raped you, even though after the incident you allowed this guy to take you home. Then even when you got home, you never came into the police station or called us. Is that what you're saying?"

I just dropped my head. Once again I had gotten in my own way. As big, bad, and tough as I thought I was, when I needed to be strong, I was weak.

The officer scolded, "You should have come and gotten a rape kit. After all this time, there is no evidence. Even the video you're talking about … did you bring it here so we can have it analyzed to see if he altered it in any way?"

"What are you saying, sir? That I wasn't raped?" I cried.

He looked at me with cold eyes and commanded, "Calm down, miss. I just want to make sure that you know what you're doing. Rape is a serious allegation."

"Raping someone is a serious crime," I responded boldly. "I was traumatized, sir. I can't explain why I didn't come forward other than to say I was scared. That might be a pathetic excuse, and I know it seems convenient that I want to talk now, but this guy is a monster and needs to be stopped. If you don't want to help me—"

Before I could finish, the door opened and there was a lady standing there. "I hear there is a young lady reporting a rape. John, I can take over from here."

"Oh no. He's made it pretty clear that I have no case," I cried. "I have only myself to blame."

"No, I didn't say that," Officer Crowell insisted. Like he was on my side. Right.

"John, you didn't tell her that, did you?"

I looked at him like, *Be real, man. You basically said that. I dare you to tell this woman that it is not what you said.* Seeing that he was not going to confess, I stood to my feet.

"I've had enough. I'm not going to be humiliated any more. I made my decision even though it was a bad one. I am the one who decided to keep it all to myself. I'll have to live with this," I said. I tried leaving the cold interrogation room.

"Wait, please, I would like to talk to you," the nicer lady said.

"Talk to him. He knows everything," I said before fleeing out the front doors of the police station.

My friends asked a million questions. I just put my hands over my ears. My head was killing me. This was too much, and I was too stressed out.

"Talk to us. Eva, you got to talk to us. You have to say something," Charli said.

"They didn't believe me, okay? I waited too long. It was my fault," I finally told them.

Charli would not let up. "Well, let's go by a hospital. You can't just give up."

"The way I feel right now, Charli, I have no fight in me. You guys be better than me, okay? No short dresses, no low-cut shirts, no wearing shirts without bras, and wear your panties at all times," I ordered.

"It wasn't your fault," Randal responded.

"Yeah, you didn't deserve this, sis," Ella said.

"Where is his tail? Let's go kill him," Charli commanded.

In a tired voice, I said, "You guys, it's late. We all need to be somewhere safe and not on the streets trying to get revenge on some guy who, according to the cops, doesn't deserve it. I know you can't understand it, but I'm tired. Please, just let me be. Just drop it. Leave me alone about it, please."

The ride back to my place was one that we made in silence. Rico took so much from me. I saw no way I could ever get it back.

"Why am I even here?" I thought to myself. I sat in the pew at Lakeside Baptist Church on Sunday morning.

My mom worked all night and got me and my sister up to go to church. She was taking all that I was going through personally. I guess she thought it was possible to pray my troubles away. I told them I needed to go to the ladies room, but I made my way into the smaller sanctuary within the mega-church.

I did not know if I believed in God or not. I never called on Him before, but I figured now was the time to try out some force bigger than myself. I needed a change of heart. I needed a change of mind. I needed a change to my soul because everything in me felt so dark and desolate.

I did not know how to pray. Honestly, I was not really feeling it. I was just thankful for the darkness. I placed my head on the pew in front of me to rest. Before I could express any kind of emotion, the door opened. I was freaking out because there were too many shadows. I could not see a clear image. I did not know who was there. I did the only thing I knew to do: hide. I saw a faint image sit in the pew in front of me. I eased up some when I heard weeping. It was not a female voice. It wasn't an older voice.

It was a young guy calling out, "Why? Why did this have to happen to me? I was so young, and I didn't do anything wrong. I tried to pretend it didn't happen, but I know it did. Why weren't You there? Why wasn't my father there? No one protected me, and now I got to deal with this alone."

After listening, I realized it was Landon's voice. What was he talking about? What did he have to live with? Why was he so upset?

Landon continued, "He touched me. He violated me. He molested me."

"Dang, what!?" I screamed. I was unable to hold back the way the words affected me.

"Who's there?" Landon demanded in a surprised-upset tone rolled into one.

"I'm … I'm sorry," I said quickly. I felt terrible that I'd inadvertently invaded his private space.

Unlike me, Landon was very familiar with the church; after all, his dad was the pastor. He ran to the back of the room and flicked on a light. He was stunned to find me there.

"You?" Landon growled in an irritated voice. "What are you doing in here, Eva?"

I walked toward him, wanting to wipe his eyes. Landon was always a jokester, the man who made the room light up, the optimist, and the one full of energy. Now his world seemed as dark as mine.

I kept walking toward him and said, "You know why I'm here. The whole school does. I don't know if I'm getting anything out of it. I don't even know how to talk to God but listening to you—"

"I can't believe you were eavesdropping." He turned away.

Turning him back toward me, I grabbed the little spunk I had left and said, "I mean, you just came in here, and you didn't ask if there was anybody else in here. Technically, this was my space before it was yours."

He huffed and realized he had the wrong one on the wrong day. "Okay, calm down. I'm not saying you shouldn't be in here. I just wish you would've told me before I start telling all of my life, like I wanted anybody to know."

"I understand. I don't exactly get what happened to you. That is your business. But I do apologize for being so caught up in everything and not letting you know I was in here, but something terrible happened to me too. I don't just mean the video that's been floating around. Something far worse, Landon. I was scared. I didn't know who was coming in. I'm just not the same anymore." I sighed, backed up, and lowered my head.

"You can't sleep?" he asked in a manner that connected to my pain.

"Nor eat," I replied.

"Or relax," he said.

"Yeah," I responded, knowing he was getting what I was going through so much that I knew we were in the same gloomy place.

He stepped closer to me, and he could see I was fragile too. "Do you want to talk?"

"I don't know," I said as tears pooled in my eyes.

"I understand," he said. A single tear fell from his eye.

I stepped closer. Seeing him crying bothered me. I wiped his face.

"Maybe we should," I said. His tears touched me to my core.

"Maybe we should what?" he asked, trying to be strong.

"Open up to each other," I stated. I truly wanted to connect. "You already know a little about what I'm going through, but you don't fully understand it. I don't even understand it, and I hope you can't relate to it. I was raped."

"Nah, Eva, don't even tell me that. Talk to me. Tell me what happened."

The way he said it connected to my heart. It was not a demand, but I could feel his need.

I had the same one: wishing that I was not in this alone, wishing that I had someone who understood, and needing someone to bounce it all off of who could rationalize it. I longed for someone to make sense of it for me, someone who truly understood. Maybe Landon was that person. Maybe I came to that small sanctuary to find a friend. Both of us sat in the back pew.

I started. "The guy who sent that video … I went out on a date with him. He wanted to take things further than I did. I said no, but he didn't listen. He edited that video to make it look like I wanted it, but I didn't. I don't know why that happened to me, but it woke me up. I was not taking life seriously. Now I'm fully conscious of my choices."

"I understand," Landon affirmed. "We got a substitute teacher who was at our school."

"Yeah," I said, remembering Mr. Gunn, the cute guy who subbed in math class.

Landon started talking in a serious tone. "He was my little league football coach when I was ten. He took me to games. He bought me ice cream after practice when my dad was just building this facility. My father was so busy, but the coach made time for me always. My dad was so grateful he never even questioned. He never even asked what we did. In middle school, I never even played football because I was so traumatized by something that happened to me in the fifth grade."

"No, please don't let Landon say that Gunn raped him," I thought, but I knew what was coming. I couldn't interrupt Landon; he let me have *my* say.

He was talking. He was sharing, and I needed to care. Unfortunately, he confirmed my worst fears. He did understand what I was going through. We had both been violated. We had both been taken advantage of. What I didn't know was, where did each of us go from here? Could either of us ever heal? I knew we were both very broken.

CHAPTER 6

Resolve Errors

You didn't have to take me to breakfast, Landon," I said as the two of us sat in a nearby Waffle House.

We had both needed to get out of that church. Neither of us wanted to go back into the service, even though some positive words may have helped.

"It's the least I could do for ... never mind," Landon responded.

Without thinking, I placed my hand on his. He gripped it real tight. We held a stare that connected somewhere deep down.

Letting go of his hand, I said, "I'm glad we can talk."

Landon said, "Yeah, it's good to open up. It's been a lot seeing that man hanging around my little brother's football team and having to confront my own memories that I tried to suppress. I don't want this to come out. I don't want to give any of my friends a reason to ask me if I'm gay. Unlike my boys, I haven't had a steady girlfriend yet."

"Well, since this has happened to me, I know what you mean about people hearing what they wanna hear and making assumptions," I said. "It's the same with me. People think because I dress a certain way or talk a certain way or—"

"Went out with a bunch of college guys," Landon cut in.

I couldn't get mad. The shoe fit and I had to wear it. My reputation was less than stellar. Now I wanted the way people viewed me to change for the better.

"Why wouldn't you ever give us guys in your grade a chance?" Landon asked.

I blurted out, "Because you all seem so immature."

"Wow, you're talking about me now," Landon teased, flexing his muscles.

I smiled, "I guess I missed the fact that some of you have grown up."

He smiled back. Landon had me blushing. This was crazy and awkward. To avoid the weird moment, we kept eating. Both of us were chowing down. All we had been going through lately, neither of us had probably eaten a lot. It was showing, as our food was gone in no time.

"What now?" I said to him. We sat there contemplating our lives, both wanting to get up out of the pit.

"I gotta talk to my dad. This all needs to come out. I want him to hear it from me. I don't know how he's gonna react. I wished worrying about his reaction didn't bother me, but it does."

"I know what you mean. My dad hates my guts right now. That's killing me," I confessed.

"Your dad just got married. I saw you here for his wedding. Weren't you standing up there with him? You had on your dress and stuff."

I wanted to comment, "You noticed that?" But then I remembered, when I bumped into him, he seemed pretty irritated. Now his demeanor made sense. Landon was not being a jerk or being rude, he actually was dealing with so much. And through all of that he remembered running into me.

As if reading my mind, he said, "I'm sorry. The couple of times I saw you in school and at the church, I wasn't even looking where I was going. Dumb me bumped straight into you. Forgive me. You now understand why I was so stressed out and preoccupied."

This guy was being nice to me. We were talking. He was caring. I didn't deserve that. I could not face him.

He turned my face toward his and said, "You know you didn't bring anything that happen to you on yourself, right? I mean, I hear you joking about your clothes and your attitude and how others perceive you. You got the right to say no. You're able to change your mind."

"Obviously, I wasn't."

"No, obviously he didn't *hear* you. Now you gotta take care of that. Your parents know?"

"My mom does."

"You call the police yet?"

"Ha-ha," I laughed.

It was not funny. However, I could not stop laughing. Police were supposed to be helpful.

The ones I dealt with were the ones who needed to not be in law enforcement.

"Talk to me," he said in a gentle way.

"I didn't go to the police right away, and when I did, I got a jerk of a cop who said I had no claim since I waited."

"What?!"

"My dad's an attorney. If I could just talk to him, maybe he could see if there's something legally I could do. I don't want Rico to be able to do this to anyone else. I couldn't stand it if he attacked someone else, and I never reported what happened to me."

"Rico. I remembered him from school a couple of years ago. What a jerk. I don't understand why people don't go away for college. I lived in the ATL all my life. While it's always gonna be in my blood, there's more to the world than here."

We were done with our delicious meal. Church was letting out, but Landon wasn't walking inside. He huffed. I realized I did not want him to struggle with confronting this anymore.

I held his hand and said, "Let's go talk to your dad. After we talk to him, you can help me talk to mine. Deal?"

He looked over at me and asked, "You'd do that?"

"We can keep each other calm. Together, rational heads prevail, right?"

"Both Rico and crazy Gunn need to be in orange jumpsuits," Landon joked. "Meet me at my dad's office in ten, okay?"

Watching him walk away, I was thankful for my new buddy. I needed to find my mom and sister so I could meet back up with Landon. As soon as I found them, my mom threw her arms around me.

My mom said, "Are you okay, sweetie?"

Nodding, I said, "Yes, ma'am. I'ma catch up with you guys later. I'm going to talk to Pastor King."

"How are you going to get home?" Ella asked. "And can you even see Pastor King?"

"Landon said he'd bring me, and I'm going to talk to his dad with him," I explained.

"Oh yes. Oh, that's good, talk to the pastor," my mom said. She hugged me before walking over to one of her friends.

"Landon knows?" my sister leaned over and whispered.

"Long story."

"Well, it seems like a good story. You're a lil' perked up. You've got pep in your step. You wanna talk to the pastor. I'm all for whatever Landon said to get you in this mood. He's a great guy—Leo's best friend. You have no issues from me." Ella grinned.

I could tell she was thinking something more than was there. I threw up my hand and turned to head out. Landon was turning out to be cooler than I thought.

My sister was also right about asking me if I could get to see Pastor King. When I got to his office, it was like a whole other complex. Getting in was like Fort Knox or something. Armor bearers and the three secretaries were all looking at me like, *Ahh, why are you up here?* This was church, and I was sure my pastor preached a great sermon. Why couldn't I just say thank you for blessing me? Did I need an appointment and status to be able to do that?

"She's with me, you guys," Landon said, rescuing me from the wolves.

They parted and let me pass. Landon grabbed my hand and pulled me. The next thing

I knew, we were sitting in a beautiful, lavish space.

"Okay, son, you know I'm preaching in Savannah. I must get on the road in a minute. What's this about?" Pastor King said from behind his large mahogany desk.

"Dad, you're not going to say hello to my friend Eva?"

Pastor noticed me for the first time. "Hello, Eva. Please forgive me for being so rude. My son said he had something to talk to me about. He steps in, then out, and then you come in. Is this about you two?"

I thought, "Sir, why can't people talk to you? Why can't people have easier access to you? Why do you make it so difficult? Why couldn't you preach at my dad's wedding? Why aren't you more involved in your son's life? He's breaking, and you can't even see it. What good does it do to be famous and inspire lots of people, when you have no follow-up and are not truly making an impact on anyone?" But I sat there, smiled, and gave the politically correct response.

"Hello, sir. No, this is just about Landon. I'm only here for support," I said. Landon's father immediately became concerned and sat to hear from his son.

All the harsh things I thought about Pastor King being too busy for the world changed in a blink of an eye. When Landon opened up and told his dad his story, his father became shaken with grief over what he heard. My heart went out to both of them.

"I'm gonna cancel my plans for today. We're gonna deal with this right now," Pastor King commanded.

"No, Dad, go preach," Landon replied, knowing his dad was important to many. "Besides, I need to go somewhere with Eva."

Pastor King came over to his son and placed his hand on his shoulder. "My boy, I should have known. I should have been there. I'm sorry."

About an hour later, Landon dropped me off. My story didn't end as well as his did. Landon thought it was best if I call my dad first before we went over there. My dad and Samantha were not even home. They had taken the baby to Samantha's relatives.

When we finally spoke on the phone, my dad didn't believe me when I said I was raped.

He accused me of concocting another ploy to try to get close to him and cause problems in his marriage. This devastated me.

Landon repeatedly tried telling me it was not my fault and it would be okay. He also said he wanted to help me through all this. Problem was, I thought it *was* my fault. My rep was so bad that even my dad did not believe me. How could Landon help me? Frustrated, I got out of the car and slammed the door. I didn't even look back at Landon, thank him, or nothing. As kind as he had been, that was not right. But that was real.

We had an away game at our rival's school not too far away. Mays High School had a rich tradition in the city of Atlanta. They had a good football team this year. However, our boys were ready to beat them. I was not ready to cheer.

My mother contacted Coach Woods and explained to her everything that had happened to me, just in case I had a meltdown. My four besties, including my sister, said they would take my secret to their graves. As I looked at each of them, I could tell it was only a matter of time before one of them popped. It was not a situation where they wanted to spread my business and hurt me. No, it was quite the opposite. They wanted to protect me. When we walked to the bathroom, we could hear crowds of people whispering about me.

"That's that girl in the video," one girl smirked.

"Yeah, she was doing all kinds of things I didn't even know people could do," another one joked.

"Look here, shawty, I wanna talk to you," one guy called out. But I briskly moved by. "Oh, don't walk away like you all that now. We done seen everything."

There was one nasty comment after another. I wrongfully assumed at an away game that I would not have to be in front of my peers, but because this was Mays, it seemed everyone from Lockwood was there. I felt everyone was ragging on me.

Thankfully, the game was going good. The Lions were kicking on all cylinders, and the defense was keeping Mays from scoring. Special teams were putting us in great field position, and Waxton was doing his thing, running the ball. That running also ran the clock down, which was really good for me. I felt like a punching bag, there for anybody who wanted to take a shot at me. My girls were getting tired of it.

Charli came over to me and said, "People need to know what happened to you. If they did, they would keep their mouths shut, but they don't and you're not gonna tell them."

We walked to the bus after we won 18–3. We made three touchdowns. The only flaw on our team was that our kicker couldn't get the extra points. We had a new guy who everyone said supposedly was great at kicking. He had NFL potential, but he wasn't eligible *and* he was white. Being white wasn't a bad thing, but he just seemed uncomfortable at our predominately black school. Randal even tripped sometimes about feeling uneasy being more than one race. I didn't see the big deal with her argument. Anytime you had a little bit of chocolate in you, the world considered you black.

I wanted to be home and put the covers over my head. So nobody could see me. So nobody knew what I was going through. So nobody could get in my case. I knew I had to open my mouth and help others, but I couldn't.

I saw a girl walking with a guy who was grabbing on her. Though she jerked away, he continued. Then there was a freshmen flirting with a senior. She might think it was innocent, but what if he took her up on the flirtation. She would not have a prayer. And what about the nerd in the crowd of hunks wishing he had more muscles and could have his way with the ladies? I wanted to scream out, "Don't rush it! You'll mature in time."

People had to stop thinking they were entitled to pressure people to give them what they wanted, and to be so dominant that they became violent. I was so choked up with these new realizations that I could not speak. I got on the bus and rode home in silence.

As soon as we got off the bus, the fall night air felt so good on my face. I just ran. I forgot I needed a way home. I forgot the lights in our stadium were off. I forgot that what I was doing there made no sense. I needed to think. Placing my head on the steel stadium bleachers, I took a rest for a second. I wanted my life to be better.

I heard my sister call out, "Eva, please. Where are you?"

Leo was with her and he shouted. "Eva! We're looking for you. Just let us know you're all right."

Then I jumped as someone touched me. I felt a strong arm against my shoulder. I turned around, ready to sock the guy. It was Landon. I exhaled deeply.

"What's going on with you? Why do you have us all worried?"

Landon sat down beside me, and I buried my head in his chest and said, "I just can't take this. It hurts so bad. I was the strongest person I knew, Landon. Now I feel like an infant. Every little thing somebody says bothers me. I hate myself. I don't know how to resolve any of this."

"Well, acknowledging your feelings is the first step. Running away is not gonna solve crap," Landon maintained. I tried to pull away, but he held me tight. "Look, I told you I'm gonna be there for you."

"How can you help me when you're sinking too?"

"Let's get in that boat, patch the thing up, and help each other survive," Landon suggested. "I'm down if you're down."

I was hesitant. "I don't know if I want everybody knowing about this. Leo's out here helping find me. He must know something is wrong. He's your boy and my sister's boyfriend. What does he know?"

"I don't know, but I haven't told him nothing. If he knows anything, it's 'cause your sister probably needed someone to talk to, and with you shutting everybody out, can you blame her? All guys aren't bad, Eva. Don't go through this alone."

"You're sweet to wanna help," I affirmed. But I backed away, knowing that the two of us couldn't be anything more than just friends. We were both too fragile for anything else. I didn't want to give him the wrong idea. His friendship was enough.

Sensing I was overwhelmed, the caring hunk in front of me said, "Let's just get out of this dark stadium. Take it one day at a time."

"I feel so unworthy to keep going on. You just don't understand," I said, explaining more than I had ever verbalized to anyone else.

"What? You wanna take your own life or something?" Landon asked. "It's not a new thought."

"You wanted to do that?" I asked.

"I gave a lot of thought to it. But where's the justice in that? What would that solve? That would give him even more power, which he doesn't deserve," Landon explained in a sweet tone. "But, Eva, we might be a little cowardly, but we are probably more courageous than we know. We just need to open up our mouths and roar to fight back the demons inside. We just need to keep building ourselves up when we wanna tear ourselves down. If we focus on the truth and not on the lies ... If we focus on the healing and not on the pain ... If we focus on what's in front of us and not what's behind ... We can be stronger because of it and help others so they won't have to go through it. One of these days we'll say it was worth it."

"That's a day I can't see right now," I whispered.

"Here, let me lend you my glasses."

"You're not wearing any," I laughed.

"See, why you have to call me out on that? I thought I was."

We both smiled. I didn't even realize we were walking toward the parking lot because I was so in tune with what he was saying. Suddenly, Landon gently kissed my forehead. We were both a little shocked at the gesture. But then I smiled at him. When my sister saw me, she rushed up and hugged me like she had not seen me in weeks. Landon was talking to Leo. I looked over at my new friend and was grateful. He was right. I had the power to get over this. It was a mind thing, and I was going to win the battle within.

It is a wonderful thing to get a good night's rest. Landon helped me put things into perspective. I was only a victim if I wanted to stay a victim. If I wanted to triumph, that could be my fate as well. And that was the direction I was choosing.

Funny thing, though. As soon as you get ready to look at life in a positive direction, something smacks you dead in the face. It tells you it ain't gonna be that easy just moving on. I thought I could remember that night with Rico in vivid detail, but then there were patches that were vague. I recalled that Rico did not use protection, and that he made sure he had a real good time.

Was I safe from getting pregnant? Safe from getting a disease? I didn't know.

Immediately, I pulled my calendar from my purse and looked at the date of when my cycle should be coming on. There were two days to go, which meant I was with Rico in the middle of my cycle, and that was the danger zone. Heck, all of it was a danger zone.

I was beginning to freak out. I did feel like I normally do when it's time for my cycle. I was irritable, a little bloated, a bit tired, and my breasts were tender. The problem was, those were the same signs as the early stages of pregnancy. I was not nauseous, but would it be too early for that? Ugh, I was freaking myself out, which was crazy.

Quickly, I went to the bathroom because I just wanted to let out everything bad in me. I did not know what I was thinking because it was not like that was possible. If I was pregnant, using the restroom would not make that go away. But there I was on the toilet, trying nonetheless.

I started feeling really weird between my legs. It was a feeling I never felt before. On one side, I was raw. When I did a self-check, there was a raised bump, which hurt extremely bad. I didn't know what to do. I didn't know what it was, but my mom was home and so was my sister.

Ella seemed so fragile. Every time I talked to her about anything, she would go into panic mode. But I was panicking too. What if I had HIV? If that was the case, the best chance I had for living was early detection and getting some medication.

I came into my room after washing my hands, closed the door, and said to Ella, "Okay, I need you to stay calm."

"What?" she croaked.

"Something's not right. Something's feeling really weird. I need to talk to Mom, but I don't wanna freak her out either."

Ella's voice rose. "What are you talking about? What's going on?"

I shared my concerns and observations about my body. She went to the laptop in the kitchen and began to surf the Internet. She wanted answers.

After a while, she came back and said, "I don't know. It could be a whole bunch of stuff. You need to talk to Mom. She needs to check you out."

"Ugh, she hasn't checked me out since I was five. She's gonna make me go to some gynecologist, and I don't want nobody putting any cold, sterile metal in places it's not supposed to go. You know what I'm saying?"

"Listen, Eva, if something is going on with you, you need to find out what it is. It's Saturday morning, and Mom probably knows a clinic that's open."

"Huh?" I didn't want to go to the clinic. "No, forget it," I said.

"What's this about a clinic?" my mom passed our room and asked. I gave my sister a hard stare.

"Talk to me, girls. Who needs a doctor?"

Ella looked straight at me. "She needs to talk to you."

My mom then came in the room. "Eva, what's going on?"

Knowing my mother was not going to let up, I said, "I don't know, Mom. I just don't feel good down there. My period is due in a couple of days. But something feels weird."

"Mom, she said she's got a bump or sore or something *down there*. You need to check her out right now, Mom. Check her," Ella insisted.

She was starting to panic, and I was incapable of speaking for myself.

My mom wasted no time making a phone call, setting up an appointment, and getting me in to see a doctor. While I waited to see the doctor, I had some tests done. I hated having on the white paper gown and sitting on a cold table. The least you think the doctor would do was have the room warm.

Mom and Ella were with me the whole time. My mom made me laugh, saying, "Ah, Miss Ella, you have a boyfriend now. Do I have to get you checked out too?"

Ella's brown face turned red. She wasn't doing nothing, and I could tell. I just cracked up at her embarrassment.

"And why are you laughing?" my mom said to me. "Because I'm dead on?"

"No, because you're *so* far off," Ella cried. She did not want to be viewed as a bad girl.

"I'm not way far off. I seen how you have been looking at Leo," my mom said, sounding like a good girlfriend.

My sister had pretty much lost her mind for the guy, but I didn't have a problem with it because he was treating her right. Everybody knew he was crazy about her too. Funny thing was, Leo had never settled down until Ella. Although they were young, you could tell they were really into each other.

"Good," my mom said. "Keep the legs closed."

Hating where we were, I said, "Right, 'cause she's got enough to deal with with my legs open."

"Eva!" Mom scolded.

I didn't have to respond because the doctor came in. The way Dr. Frost was looking, I thought she was about to confirm I was either pregnant or dying. So I asked her if was I either. Then a smile brushed across her face.

The doctor became serious. "It's still a little early to tell if you are pregnant, even though we gave you the test. Thus far it is negative. And you're not dying. The bad news is you do have a venereal disease. It's called herpes, and it will not go away."

"What do you mean? I'm gonna have this sore forever?" I cried.

"Well, not in the form it is currently in. You'll have to take medication to keep it under control.

Some are taken orally, and there are also creams that will make the sore more bearable. Don't wear tight clothes because that will irritate it. When you don't take the medicine, an outbreak will come up. We don't know why the disease flares, and there are some reasons we don't understand."

"Will the sore always be in the same place?" I sobbed.

"It could, but it could also move around. You could have multiple sores. Thankfully, you caught this early. Do you know you are able to pass this on to others as well?"

"What?"

"Yes, if you feel a little irritable, it's the outbreak at its full stage, and you're contagious."

My mom stood up and hugged me tight.

"I recommend you get some counseling, and I'd like to see you in a couple weeks to test you again for some other things. I know this is hard and seems unfair with what you went through, but everyone goes on and lives healthy lives with this virus. I know you will too. It was a terrible thing that happened to you, but right now, the best thing we can do is get you treated, get you healthy, and resolve errors."

CHAPTER 7

Blissful Truth

Okay, you guys, you don't have to fuss over me so," I commanded. My mother and sister were attending to my every need and driving me crazy.

My sister propped up my feet and said, "We just want to make sure you're comfortable."

My mom came and put a pillow behind me. "You've been through a lot," she sighed. "You deserve some pampering." Then she started massaging my back. She bent down and kissed me on the cheek. My sister took off my slippers and rubbed my feet through my socks.

"Okay, you guys," I giggled. "I'm okay, really."

It was Sunday evening. The school week was about to get started, but just having two days of whatever the medicine was called that the doctor gave me for my disease was helping. My mom and sister were making sure I was not stressed out. That was another thing the doctor said that would flare up an outbreak.

There was a knock on the door. My mother looked at my sister and said, "Now? It's nine. It is too late for Leo to be trying to come over here."

"That shouldn't be him, Mom. It's not Dr. Sapp, is it?" Ella teased.

"Wait, what? Am I missing something?" I questioned, knowing the last couple of weeks I'd been out of it.

My mom could have had lunch with Mrs. Obama, and I wouldn't have noticed the Secret Service come to pick her up. I was just that dazed. I had gone through a ton. The only person's business I could handle was my own.

"What are you talking about, Ella?" our mom, sounding very innocent, asked.

"Our principal's got the hots for our mom," Ella leaned over and told me.

"*I knew it*," I said, remembering him eyeing her like she was a biscuit dipped in hot gravy or something.

"I just invited him to Thanksgiving," Mom dismissed "Nothing more."

"Yeah, and ever since then you've been going around here cleaning, putting up drapes, and making this place a home," Ella replied. It was looking like HGTV in our apartment.

My mom replied, "We needed to fix it up. No big deal."

Ella chuckled. "Okay, if that's how you want to play it, fine with me."

Then the knock came again. The talk about Dr. Sapp made us forget that someone was even at the door. The three of us wondered who it was.

"Maybe that's our principal," I called out, playing with my mom.

"Yeah, maybe it is," Ella teased. My mom gave us a look that said, *Enough!*

Things were going really well for me until I saw my mother open the door. My dad was standing there with Samantha. What did *they* want? Were they coming over here to gloat? I had not seen him since he went off on me at the football game. Did he want to tell me off in front of her because she did not believe that he had taken care of the problem—me? If I had on jeans, I would have gone to my room, but I had on big boxers, so I just sat there, pulled the covers closer, and held a defiant glare.

"May we come in?" my dad asked my mom.

My mom could tell I was not feeling them. She said, "Eva's resting. We certainly would've loved to know you were coming. She's not really fully dressed."

Surprisingly, Samantha stepped forward and said, "It's my fault. This is impromptu. I really wanted to come by."

"I wanted to come by too," my dad concurred. "We were nearby, and we really want to speak to Eva, if that's okay."

"Where's my little brother?" Ella said to the newlyweds.

"Do you mean Evan or El?"

"Oh my gosh! The baby's name is similar to mine," Ella cried. She rushed to them for hugs.

Good for her, she was friends with the two of them. I really could not relate to either one of them, regardless of the fact that one was my father. My dad said something to my mom because Mom and Ella disappeared into the kitchen.

Not wanting to be alone with my dad and his bride, I quickly uttered, "You didn't have to come all the way over here, Dad. You could've put Samantha on the phone, and I would've told her that you went off on me and told me to never bother y'all again. Now if that's it, I'd like to rest."

Teardrops were visible in Samantha's eyes. "I came to ask you to forgive me."

Truly surprised and confused, I murmured, "Huh?"

Samantha continued, "I should've known you were so similar to me. Spunky, sassy, attractive, indiscreet, flashy, showing poor judgment, and then letting all of that backfire in your face."

Where was Samantha going with this? I did not understand what she was trying to say to me. She was getting really emotional with me, and whatever it was about, it seemed pretty serious.

"When your dad told me what happened to you … it brought up a lot of bad memories for me. When I was in college, I was extremely popular. I was a majorette in the band at Howard. I never pledged a sorority; those girls hated on me a little too much."

"Just tell her," my dad interrupted because Samantha was going all the way around the world just to get to some point.

"There was this guy who already graduated and was interning with the legislature. He told me he could help move my career forward. He told me that he could get me a job in the White House. He was going to help me with my résumé. I admit, I liked him at first, but he took things too far, too fast. I tried to break things off. Things got ugly, and I was never the same." She sat down on the sofa next to me and held my hand. "What happened to you was not your fault. I didn't even have to know all the details, but I believe you one hundred percent. I'm sorry I didn't tell you my story, because I saw where you were headed. Women have to do a better job of encouraging one another. You trusted the wrong guy, and it cost you. Back then, I didn't know legal folks. Now, I am in the legal profession. I want to help you. I work for the district attorney. We can prosecute the horrible guy who did this."

My dad said, "I should've believed you too, pumpkin. I was just so clouded by my own mistakes that I didn't see what you were saying.

I am your father, but I wasn't there for you. I know that you've been doing outlandish things because you were starved for attention from your father. I just wasn't there for you," he repeated. "I'll never be able to make that up to you."

"Daddy, you don't have to say that," I exclaimed. Their empathy was affirming and overwhelming.

At that moment, I was really grateful that I had two lawyers who believed me. My dad had not been there during my upbringing. However, he was standing before me in my time of need. I reached up and hugged him.

"We're going to get him," my dad declared. Then he tightened the embrace we shared.

I pulled back as I remembered I'd already tried this and was unsuccessful. "I don't know how. I went to the cops, and they told me I had no evidence."

"Yeah, you told me that, but you said there was some tape going around. We just need to get a copy of that," my father said.

Samantha looked at me and said, "Look, I know it's been rough with people accusing you of bringing this on yourself and others not believing your story. Dealing with this internally has to be so difficult. It took me years to get better because I had no one to talk to. I know things have been rough between us, and you must feel like you've lost your father all over again. Let's scratch all that history and drama. Let's start from the beginning … from a place of love. Because if you're okay with it, I want to make sure you have everything you need to overcome this."

Ready to start anew with my stepmother, I reached up and hugged her. I could see my dad over her shoulder, and I mouthed, "Thank you." Rico took a lot from me, and now it seemed like I was starting to get some great things back.

We were having two assemblies at school as part of the Stand Against Violence Campaign. The school district brought in a team of professionals from around the country to talk to us about bullying, gang violence, self-mutilation, and rape. The boys were going to be in the gym, and the girls were in the auditorium. Almost everybody was excited because nobody had to be in class. I was not as thrilled to go hear a bunch of people talk about these tough subjects.

But we did have an out. If you did not want to attend the assembly, you could go to the library and study. Since Ella showed me how to buckle down and really study, I realized I was doing myself an injustice by not working hard in school. I was caught up with my work, but I could've read ahead or gone over some things that I missed; however, as much as I did not want to be in the auditorium and talk about violence, I had an overwhelming feeling that I really did need to be there.

Someone touched my waist and I jerked. I looked around and saw it was Landon. My fist was about to hit him.

"I'm sorry. I'm sorry," he apologized.

"Boy, you scared me!"

"I was just playing."

"Playing? You know I'm on edge."

"Right, sorry, I wasn't thinking," he said. "You doing okay?"

"Mr. King and Miss Blount, y'all need to get where y'all are supposed to be and pronto," Dr. Sapp barked.

"See you later," Landon whispered.

Before I went into the auditorium, Dr. Sapp said, "Tell your mom I'm looking forward to Thanksgiving dinner."

"Oh, I'll tell her," I said slyly. I wanted to tell him that she was looking forward to it too. Something was definitely going on there.

There was a panel made up of three professionals in the assembly: one lady was a psychologist, another lady was a policewoman, and the third was a medical doctor. We were not guys, but everyone was so loud and hyped up. Girls were being rude to the presenters and not even paying attention to the good information that was being shared.

Dr. Sapp was not in there with us because he was with the boys. Our assistant principal was in the back, but no one respected him because he was such a wimp. He tried to get people to calm down, but folks got louder.

Finally, I just stood and hollered, "Hey, everyone calm down. They're trying to help you. They're trying to tell you stuff that you need to hear. You guys need to calm down and listen."

"What do you care?" somebody yelled out.

"Yeah, tramp, what do you know about it with the way you give it up?" another person hollered.

"I know a lot about it, okay?"

"Young lady?" one of the speakers interrupted. "Would you like to come up front and tell your story?"

Ella was sitting next to me. She tugged on my jacket and said, "You don't have to."

I turned to her and declared, "I want to."

As I walked to the stage, the medical doctor gave statistics. "Did you know one in seven students in grades K–12 are either a bully or a victim of bullying. It is estimated that one hundred sixty thousand children miss school daily because of the fear of violence or intimidation by other students. A review of surveys found that between thirty and forty percent of male teens and sixteen to thirty-two percent of female teens say they have committed a serious violent offense by the age of seventeen. Another staggering statistic is that suicide is the third leading cause of death among teenagers. Over fifteen hundred teens kill themselves each year."

The policewoman, who looked familiar, added, "Yes, more than three in five youth suicides involve firearms. Every two minutes someone in America is being sexually assaulted, and every year there are about two hundred thirteen thousand victims of sexual assault. Forty-four percent of rape victims are under age eighteen and eighty percent are under age thirty. Fifty-seven percent of the rapes happened while on dates. Sixty percent of sexual assaults are not reported to police, and fifteen out of sixteen rapists will never spend a day in jail. Approximately two-thirds of assaults are committed by someone known to the victim, and thirty-eight percent of rapists are friends or acquaintances."

Charli yelled out, "Yeah, when you go to the cops and they give you a hard time, why tell? Why bother?"

The policewoman said, "Officers are not perfect. Sometimes you catch them in a tough moment. If you ever feel like one is not hearing you out, don't leave. Find another one. We do care."

I got to the stage and became timid when I looked around the room. I breathed deep and knew I had to speak up. If ever there was a time for sassy Eva to show up, it was now. If I could help someone else be wiser, I needed to.

Finding the courage, I said, "I know y'all have probably heard about or saw the sexting scandal that involved me. What you don't know is that the video was manipulated. What you actually saw was an assault. A date rape. I'm getting counseling to help me understand that it was not my fault. I said no. I just want to say to you guys that I thought I didn't need anybody to tell me anything. I thought my body was my greatest attribute, and that I needed to flaunt it to get what I wanted in this life."

I took a deep breath and continued, "I put myself in a tough situation. I went out with a guy who looked at me like all he wanted to do was have his way. I went out with him anyway, knowing that was not what I wanted. I went out with him late at night. I had skimpy clothes on. He raped me after I said no. I hurt myself. We're all getting older, and our hormones are changing. Slow your roll. Know who you're going out with. Be careful. If you end up in a situation you don't want to be in, go to the police immediately."

You could hear a pin drop in the room. Every girl had tuned in. Every girl understood how serious this was to me. Every female there knew date rape, teen violence, and self-mutilation was real and affecting girls at Lockwood High School. They needed to wake up and be more responsible. They needed to be better than I was.

The psychologist stood and said, "Thank you so much for sharing that."

As I went to my seat, I knew the girls were going to look at me differently. I knew I had put myself out there. I made myself so transparent, but that was my duty. If I could help one girl not go through what I went through, then telling the truth was worth it.

As soon as the assembly was over, I could not get out of the place. First the police officer came over and told me she remembered me and my friends coming to the station. She apologized and told me the officers had been lectured for being too cavalier.

Many girls were coming up to me and telling me their stories about how they went out with guys who they had reservations about, and now they knew not to go out with them again. Other girls, who had similar experiences to my own, were thankful that they were not alone. Many girls thanked me for my transparency.

I was happy to be making lemonade out of lemons. We females had to stick together. For so long I tried so hard to set myself apart from them, but now I knew I was one of them through and through—vulnerable, emotional, and fragile. Yet my strength was resilient, and if all girls found and lived in a healthy place, we could keep one another lifted up.

When we headed out of the assembly, Ella ran up and gave me a huge hug. "I'm so proud of you, sis. That was excellent."

"Thanks, girl," I said as I realized I needed to share with her how much she meant to me. "And thanks for being there for me. I know I haven't always been the easiest sister to have, but you're the only one I'd ever want."

Staring back at my mirror image, I hugged her so hard. She was actually the better part of me. Because I embraced that, I was becoming better.

"He asked me," Ella giggled. I could tell that she could not hold in her excitement.

"He asked you what?"

"To the homecoming dance."

"Why is homecoming at the end of our season? That is crazy," I commented.

"I know, right? My Leo asked me." Ella twirled. "At first he said he didn't want to go, but then he asked me."

"Girl, you knew he was gonna ask you, so don't even trip."

"You've got to go too," Ella responded.

Faster than a track runner takes off when the starter gun fires, I scoffed, "Uh, no."

"No, I'm serious, sis. You don't have to worry about a date or anything. You can go stag."

"Yeah, I'm thinking about going by myself," Randal interrupted. She put her arm in mine.

"It's not that; it's just that I don't wanna—"

Before I even got a chance to continue to explain my reasons why I did not want to attend, Dr. Sapp came up to me and ordered, "Eva Blount, I need to see you in my office please."

My sister, feeling giddy, pointed directly at me, making sure he did not get us confused. She did not want to go back to ISS, but I did not want to go to his office again. What had I done? It dawned on me as I walked to his office that this was about the video floating around on people's cell phones. I was ready for Dr. Sapp. Truth was, I had nothing to do with it. I had done all I could to stop it, and I did not have to defend myself.

Before I could state my case, I saw my mom. "I was so excited to see you. I just had to get you out of class. You won't believe this."

"What, Mom, what?" Then I thought to myself, "You two are getting married?"

She explained, "They arrested Rico this morning. Your dad called me. We're gonna get this thing behind you, baby. I just want to let you know the cops believe you and so does the prosecutor. Samantha came through."

"Still, Mom, I'm the only one. It'll be my word against his."

She said, "No, baby. He created that tape, and then he sent it. You are still a minor. That is against the law. He's going to get some time. Are you going to be all right if you have to testify?"

If I never had to see Rico again, I would be so relieved. However, because I knew I had to put him away, I was ready to face him. He needed to know consequences came with his evil actions.

"Yes, ma'am," I affirmed. "I am definitely ready to testify."

"That's what I'm talking about," she encouraged. "My girl! That strength and fight in you I love so much is still there."

"You love it?" I questioned, feeling like she'd always detested my ways. "I thought you hated that I was so brash and sassy."

"In everything we need moderation. Too many sweets can make you sick, but do I want you to be meek and soft spoken? No. One of us in the household with that role is enough."

We both laughed, thinking of dear Ella. "I'm proud of you, baby. Understand that you don't have to be so hard, so tough, and have the wall up so high that you end up hurting yourself."

"I know, Mom. I've learned so much. I just spoke at the assembly and talked to other girls about what I have been through."

"Wow, you did? That was so brave, honey."

"Yeah, at first I didn't want to, but I figured if I could help anyone else be smarter and wiser, then maybe that's why I went through all of this. My reputation was shot anyhow; everyone's gonna look at me cross-eyed."

"So what? You're a wonderful person to put everyone else's needs over your own. I was behind you whether you decided to keep this to yourself or shout it from the rooftops, but I think this is a great decision. You blessed others, and that's always a good thing."

"So why do I care about how they perceive me or how they look at me or what they think about me? Ugh, Mom, none of this was ever me. Now I'm not so tough."

"Baby, you're tougher than you think. To actually stand up for what you believe in is laudable. If I had a medal, I'd give it to you, but for now I'll just give you another hug. Can I do that?"

"Yes, ma'am," I laughed.

I saw Dr. Sapp looking in on us. Though he had given us privacy, he was checking my mom out. I headed to the door to get to class.

"So what are you going to do about that one?" I said, indicating Dr. Sapp, who turned away quickly, trying to look like he was not looking at all.

"What do *you* think about that?" she asked.

"I know the way you've been cleaning and prepping our apartment. You like him."

She said, "Yeah, you know me, which is weird because we haven't really gotten a chance to talk."

"Go talk to him," I stated.

Surprised and smiling, she questioned, "You'd approve?"

"One thing I've learned is that you've got to take dating slow. Besides, you deserve happiness, Mom. Dr. Sapp is one of the good guys. I'll let y'all talk. I'll see you later. And thanks for telling me about the case. Things do work out."

My mom blew a kiss my way. When I exited, I smiled wildly at Dr. Sapp. I gave him a thumbs-up. He squinted. I nodded, letting him know that I knew and approved of him dating my mom.

When we got to our last class of the day, it was time to elect people for homecoming court. Of course, I put down my sister. Landon and I had English class together. Because we'd been in our own worlds for the past two weeks, I had forgotten that we were classmates until he came up to me and touched my shoulder.

"Hey."

"Hey," I said.

"Everybody's been talking about how you inspired them."

"I wasn't going to say anything, but I just felt I had to. But I think you've got something to feel good about too. I saw that math sub being removed from school first thing this morning. Was that your doing?"

"Could be." Landon looked at me with serious eyes. "Well, I know it meant something to folks for you to stand up and tell your story."

"I hope so," I told him.

"So, um, this dance next week ... are you going?"

"No, I'm still chilling. Low profile, you know. Why?" I asked, thinking he probably was not going to go either.

He said, "You know, I've just been hoping that you've been okay. It's been occupying my mind so much that I haven't even had time enough to focus on my own problems. You've been a great diversion."

"Well, I'm glad, I guess," I said.

"So I thought you could put a smile on my face if you would accompany me to the dance, but if you're not going, I can totally understand why."

"No, if you're gonna go, then I'd love to."

Our teacher allowed us to talk if we kept it low since the results of the elections would be announced before the period was over. Landon and I laughed and joked about nothing. I could not speak for him, but for me, it was the first time in a long time I felt normal. No eyes were watching me. No one was judging me. I was just a girl laughing with a guy as teens should do.

Dr. Sapp got on the intercom and announced the homecoming court. One freshman, one sophomore, and one junior would represent the court, and there were five seniors who would be up for homecoming queen with the winner being announced the night of homecoming.

I was not even paying attention but then he said, "Eva Blount, congratulations for being the junior class representative on the court."

I was blown away. Folks in my junior class picked me. I felt so unworthy. Maybe because I showed them that I was imperfect, they chose me to be their princess. Coming clean and sharing the darkest parts of me perhaps had helped others to not go down my path. My confession was rewarding for me in many ways. I would be forever changed for the better by my dark experience. While I still had a lot of healing, I knew in my heart that I *was* worthy. I was not shattered by my experience, and I took joy in that blissful truth.

STEPHANIE PERRY MOORE is the author of many YA inspirational fiction titles, including the *Payton Skky* series, the *Laurel Shadrach* series, the *Perry Skky Jr.* series, the *Yasmin Peace* series, the *Faith Thomas Novelzine* series, the *Carmen Browne* series, the *Morgan Love* series, and the *Beta Gamma Pi* series. Mrs. Moore speaks with young people across the country, encouraging them to achieve every attainable dream. She currently lives in the greater Atlanta area with her husband, Derrick, and their three children. Visit her website at www.stephanieperrymoore.com.

WANT A DIFFERENT
point of view?

JUST *flip* THE BOOK!